GEORGE SHERMAN HUDSON

LIGHTS OUT

Acknowledgements

First let me thank God for giving me the health, wisdom, and strength to bring on my next piece of work.

I also want to thank my first lady Shawna A. for being her…A Super Woman for real! G Street Entertainment… Hard work and dedication make dreams come true.

I want to thank my family for all the love and support… The Hudsons, Walkers and Adams.

To the G Street fam…we doing numbers! No question!

I want to acknowledge all my social networking family… Angels & Goon Squad and all my Twitter and Facebook fam.

Thanks to all the fans who make this all possible. We really appreciate the continued support.

~ G

This book is dedicated to...The Next Chapter
G Street Entertainment
G Street Chronicles, G Street Cinema, G Street Music

We Working!

"I don't know where it's coming from, but information from our weekly meetings is finding its way to our competition, and that's cost me over a quarter-mill," B-Low snapped as he walked around the office conference room table in his tailor-made suit, looking at each of his high-ranking members of his flourishing drug operation.

"Say, Low, lemme holla at yo' for a second," JP said. He hung up on the phone call with his street connect and walked over to the corner of the room, out of earshot.

As JP whispered in B-Low's ear, the whole crew looked on. They all noticed B-Low and JP zeroing in on Casey, the newest member to be promoted to a head position.

Casey didn't miss the connection, but he knew he wasn't the one responsible for it. "Excuse me for a second, y'all. My bladder is about to bust," he blurted out. He stood and made his move to get out of the room, but right as he reached the door, a hand on his shoulder caught his attention.

"Hold up, bro. We just got some good news, and I wouldn't want you to miss it," B-Low said in a sinister tone as he led Casey back over to his seat with a firm hand on his shoulder.

"That's what's up, bro. Don't wanna miss the news. I can hold it for a sec' or two," Casey said, trying hard not to piss on himself while wishing he hadn't drunk the two beers on the way over.

"I want to make an announcement!" B-Low said, drawing everyone's attention.

The five members watched B-Low as he walled back over to his high-backed chair at the head of the custom-made conference room table that complemented the ex-pensively furnished office located in the heart of down-town Atlanta. B-Low had come a long way in just a year. After hooking up with Juan, one of the biggest drug sup-pliers out of Jacksonville, B-Low had gone straight to the top. He'd thought he was rich when he hit his first million, but that changed when he reached the ten-million-dollar mark. B-Low now headed one of the biggest drug move-ments in the South. After taking over Atlanta and a couple surrounding cities, he brought in some of his trusted work-ers and promoted them to top positions in the organiza-tion; they supplied their assigned cities. Now that business was thriving and growing, more workers were getting promoted and more money was being made. At times, B-Low thought back to the man who'd made it all possible, Real. He'd thought Real was still serving time in a Down South prison, but what he didn't know was that Real had been out looking for him to make him pay for the death of Real's everything, Constance.

"I just got news about our current situation. We've found the rat," B-Low bellowed, smiling at his cohorts and colleagues who were sitting at the table.

Just as he made the announcement, his right-hand man JP stood and pulled his .45 automatic from his waistband; everyone else at the table was still clueless about the infiltrator.

A couple seconds later, Casey stood. "Bro, I gotta hit this bathroom right fast," he said, about to let go of his bladder.

The barrel of JP's gun connected with the side of his face before Casey ever knew what hit him.

"Ah, fuck!" Casey yelled out in pain as he stumbled back and fell over his chair.

"You bitch-ass disloyal muthafucker. I give you a respected position in my organization, and you go and betray me?" B-Low said calmly as he lifted up his wine glass and took a sip.

"Man, Low, I swear it ain't me! Please br—" Casey started, but he was cut off from speaking another whining word when the butt of JP's gun connected again; this time, it landed on his nose, instantly drawing spurts and rivers of blood from his nostrils.

"What you want to do with this nigga, Low?" JP asked as the other members looked on at the discipline being dished out on the traitor.

"You know how it goes, JP. No body, no case," B-Low said calmly. He stood to leave and dismissed all the others.

"Wait, Low! Man, I swear I—" Casey tried to protest, but JP's next blow knocked him out cold.

After everyone cleared the room, JP called in the cleaning crew, though it wasn't a regular cleaning crew. This crew worked for the organization and specialized in body removal. When they arrived on the scene, the room was empty, and Casey was lying on his stomach with his hands and legs bound.

"Got a live one here," Ranjan told Jack as they surveyed the scene.

"Hit JP back and see what's up," Jack said as he turned Casey over.

Just as Jack put his hands on the body, Casey suddenly came to and instantly started pleading. He was very familiar with the cleaning crew, and he knew that if they'd been called in, it was usually a done deal. "Look, man, I got money! I'll pay y'all! Please don—"

Crack!

Jack, an expert in martial arts, reached down and snapped the pleading Casey's neck with ease; he knew JP wouldn't ever want to spare a rat.

"Toe-tag 'im," Ranjan said after hanging up with JP.

"Done," Jack said and smiled, loving the rush he got from administering death.

"Let's clean this up," Ranjan said, pulling a pair of latex gloves from his pocket and snapping them on like a surgeon.

Disloyalty in the organization wasn't tolerated. That was exactly why JP had to be so discreet while he made all the moves he could to pull the seat right out from under B-Low.

Chapter 2

"Oh yes, baby! Oh shit! Yes! God!" Tina, the neighborhood junkie trick screamed as Real plowed into her rough and hard, all hyped up on X, gin, and cocaine.

Every since Real's release, he'd been chasing a high that he just couldn't seem to catch. Before his bid in the Georgia prison system, Real had been *the* man in the city. He owned G-Spot, the most popular strip club at the time. He had a mansion in one of Atlanta's most affluent neighborhoods, as well as a multimillion-dollar car collection that boasted Bentleys, Ferraris, and other expensive automobiles. But none of those material things, no matter their cost, could come close to the happiness that Constance, his pride and joy, had brought into his life. The lovers were engaged to be married after his release, but Constance would never have a chance to walk down that aisle; she was killed by one of Real's nemeses, mutilated like a dog in the street. The worst part of it all was that it had all been caught on

Real's voicemail. His lady's final cries would forever linger within him, fueling the rage Real harbored inside.

By the time he was released into a world without Constance, Real had basically given up on life. The only things he lived for were that next high and his chance at revenge. Real returned to the source of his past wealth, and that had changed him from the man he once was. Real consumed the white powder daily; he grew to love and crave the rush, that tingling sensation it gave him. It also took him to a faraway place where he could escape his thoughts of his loving Constance and the good life he'd once had.

"Yeah, baby! Oh yes! Throw me my pussy! Oh, I love you, Constance! Ah, yeah, it feels so...Ah! I'm cummingggg!" Real screamed as he released inside of Tina's wet spot.

"Damn, man, you good," Tina said, jutting her tongue through the empty spot in the front of her mouth that used to be home to a gold tooth.

"Wh-what? Huh? Constance?" Real spat as he sat up and looked down at the woman lying beneath him.

"Constance? Nah, baby, this Tina," she said. She smiled, displaying a mouthful of rotten black and yellow teeth.

"Bitch!" Real snapped when he realized that the used-up junkie beneath him wasn't his baby girl; Constance had been dead for at least a year.

"Hold up, man! Get up off me!" Tina screamed as she tried to wiggle out from under Real.

High on cocaine, X, and strong liquor, Real blanked out. He grabbed Tina by the neck.

"Stop! Help! Let me go!" Tina screamed, hoping someone in the hole-in-the-wall hotel room would hear her and come to the rescue.

The drugged-out bitch's screams only enraged Real more. He removed his right hand from her throat and drew back and started hitting Tina in the face with everything he had, each and every blow connecting solidly with bone and flesh.

"Ow! Please stop! Ahhh!" Tina screamed before the fourth violent blow knocked her out cold.

Real, high out of his mind, was enraged that the junkie trick had tried to masquerade as his baby Constance. Real was in a zone, and he kept beating the helpless Tina. After a few minutes of continuous blows, Real released his grip and rose up off the girl, who was now all bloody and barely breathing. He grabbed his pants and jacket, then stumbled to the door and out to his car. Still high and drunk, Real started the car and hit the gas to the floor, burning rubber on the way out of the parking lot.

He took a left onto the interstate. As he drove, rushing home to his shabbily furnished one-bedroom apartment in the poorest section of Atlanta's south side, he reflected back on it all. He had to move into that raggedy place because he'd quickly depleted his hefty offshore account, and he could no longer afford his spacious loft, the one he'd settled in when he'd first gotten out of prison. But none of that mattered to him anymore. Real was far from the man he'd been only a year ago. Now, he only wanted two things: revenge and his next high.

Chapter 3

*R*eal woke up the next morning with a splitting headache and a miserable hangover. He got out of bed and slowly walked into the bathroom and turned on the shower. As the water cascaded down his back, he thought about his life and what it had become. The same drugs that had made him millions now had him broke and busted. Real slumped under the showerhead and started to silently pray. He asked for strength to swear off the drugs that had invaded his life and made him less of a man. Then, he shook off his misery, stood erect again, and began to lather up. As he rinsed off, he thought about his mission. He knew he needed to have his money right before he went to war, so he pondered a plan to get back to the top.

Later in the day, Real grabbed his best suit out of the closet and pulled out an old pair of gators that he hadn't worn since the good old days at his G-Spot club. He was aware that money attracts money, so he knew he had to dress the part. He sat around for a couple hours until it was time to head down to City Lights, the most elegant nightclub in the city.

City Lights was nestled in the busiest part of Buckhead, and it catered to the rich and famous. The club was a much-talked-about meeting ground for the elite. Real and other men had used the facilities to conduct multimillion-dollar drug deals while sipping some of the finest champagne money could buy. That was exactly what had brought Real to the club again, and he was looking to scope out a potential victim.

He pulled into the club parking lot and found a spot around back; he knew his shabby transportation didn't exactly complement his fine suit and decent gators. As he got out and made his way across the lot, he admired all the expensive automobiles glistening in the valet parking area. Real couldn't wait to get back in power, but not just for the material things. He loved expensive cars as much as anyone else, but what he really longed for was vengeance.

"Hey, sexy," the blonde-haired black girl said as Real walked up and paid the club entrance fee.

"What up, beautiful?" Real spat back, feeling himself in his tailored pinstriped suit with the gators to match.

"Shit, just trying to make ends meet, if you know what I mean. You have a good time tonight. We may just bump into each other," she said as the next person in line slid up to pay the club admission.

"I'm gonna try to," Real replied.

Inside the club, Real knew the real heavy hitters from the little fish. The good thing about City Lights was that most of the people in attendance were heavy hitters. Real scoped out the scene, looking for a possible mark. As he looked around at the crowd, he heard a familiar voice calling out his name.

"Real!" Cream screamed, hurrying across the room toward him.

She'd been crazy about Real from day one. In fact, Constance had been the only thing that had kept Real from making the beautiful Cream his; back at the G-Spot, he'd had to fight off her temptations plenty of nights. Real couldn't help but smile as he thought about the numerous occasions when Constance had to check Cream for coming on to him.

"Cream," Real replied, barely audible. He was really surprised to see her, but she was as beautiful as ever with her light green eyes sparkling under the clubs disco ball.

"Man, it's been a long time. It's great to see you, Real!" Cream said excitedly as she reached over and pulled him into a hug.

When Real took Cream into his arms, he felt a pang of guilt, recalling how hard Constance had worked to keep that woman out of his reach. "Yeah, it's been a while," he said. "You good?" Real asked, releasing their embrace and looking her up and down, taking notice of all the huge diamonds and platinum pieces she was decked out in.

"Yeah, I'm good. I got my own call girl service now, and it's going pretty well. What are you into nowadays? You just disappeared after the club closed down. At first they said you was locked up, but then people said you'd moved out to Cali. You just fell off the face of the Earth,"

Cream said playfully, reaching over and rubbing his chest.

"That's what's up. I…" Real stopped midsentence as an old white man pulled up.

"Hey, baby. Are you gonna join us for dinner?" he asked, wrapping his arm around Cream's waist.

Real looked on, surprised, then introduced himself. "Hi. I'm Richard," he said, extending his hand.

"Hello, Richard. I'm Dan, Kim's husband," he said, firmly marking his territory.

"Yeah, she was just telling me so much about you. You know, Crea…er, uh, Kim and I go way back. We've known each other since grade school," Real said, smiling and mentally counting up the old man's net worth.

The old, gray-haired, distinguished gentleman was sporting a very expensive Carl F. Bucherer gold watch and diamond cufflinks set in gold. His perfectly tailored suit fit his slim frame to a T, and the Italian loafers he wore had more than likely been custom made, shipped in on special order. Being from money himself, Real had no problem assessing the man, from his attire to his accessories. He knew for sure, just by looking at him, that the man standing before him had to be worth millions; when it came to gold-digging, Cream had struck it rich.

"Yeah, baby, Richard and I are like family," she said, giving him her best fake smile.

"That's great. How about you join us for dinner?" Dan insisted more than asked.

"I wish I could, but I'm here on some very important business. Can I take a rain-check?" Real lightly joked.

"Sure, Ricky. That'd be great," Dan bellowed.

"Uh, that's Richard, if you don't mind," Real said. "Here's my number. Make sure y'all keep in touch," he said, more to Cream than to Dan as he handed her his contact info.

"Okay. We'll give you a call sometime," she answered, rolling her eyes as she followed behind the old white man. It was clear to everyone but her fool of a husband that she just wished he would go ahead and die so she could collect her rightful millions off him.

Real laughed and winked at Cream as she dutifully followed the old relic. Right then and there, he came up with a plan to get back on top, and Dan and his fat bank account were going to be heavily involved. What Real didn't know was that Dan wasn't just some old tycoon with leftover inheritance. In fact, good old silver-haired Dan was one of the biggest arms dealers in the U.S., very well liked and respected all over the world. Feeble as he looked, the man could end a man's life with one phone call.

Chapter 4

" *L*ook, Seth, I'm handing this nigga to you on a platter. What more do you want?" JP screamed into the phone at one of B-Low's fiercest competitors.

"You want your own pipeline, you gotta bring more to the table. Listen, I'm about to make you a very rich man who won't have to answer to nobody but me—no cartel boss, no B-Low, no police. Just me! I'm gonna give you control of territories that you could never even touch on your own. B-Low's days of glory are over. That nigga's too much of a hothead, and on top of that, he's ruffling too many feathers with the men up top, the suits and uniforms who're letting us have our way. Understand? You—not me—are gonna eliminate our little problem. I'm not using my manpower on that piece of shit, but if I have to, I'll make sure his whole organization is eliminated... and I mean everyone," Seth said as two dark, tan blondes flopped down on the pool chairs, flanking him outside of his multimillion-dollar home nestled inside of one of

Atlanta's most affluent neighborhoods.

"It's gonna be hard to pull that off. You know this nigga is protected like the Pres—" JP tried but was quickly cut off.

"Listen to me. If you want this position, you gotta get rid of him. When the job is done, contact me, and I'll set everything up for you," Seth explained as he picked up his apple martini and took a sip.

"A'ight, man, a'ight. I'll be in touch," JP said, ending the call.

What JP didn't realize was that Angela, a well-known dime-piece, a freaked-out gold-digger whom B-Low had passed along to JP months earlier, was listening in from the bedroom. Angela mentally counted the dollars she could make just by relaying the information she'd overheard back to B-Low. She knew it was her chance to get paid and to get close to the man she'd always wanted for herself; she wasn't just looking for a quickie from B-Low, but he'd always turned down her commitment invitations, even after their heated sex sessions.

JP stood in the kitchen of his townhouse, thinking hard about Seth's demands. Every since B-Low's rise to the top, he'd been treating JP like a chump. Without JP's muscle and connections back when they'd first put the organization together, B-Low wouldn't have been in the position to handle anybody like that. JP had opened doors for B-Low, doors that only made men could get in.

Even back when B-Low was a stick-up kid and hit man, he never could compare to the kid across the tracks, the kid known as JP. They'd grown up together on the west side of Atlanta, but they'd run with different crews back then. After Real had put B-Low on, B-Low didn't waste any time recruiting JP because he knew every boss needed some muscle. As soon as JP made it known in the city that he was down with B-Low, all kinds of doors began to open for B-Low, and his rise to the top took no time. Now, with all his wealth and power, he was handling JP like a do boy, just throwing him crumbs. JP had made up his mind to dethrone B-Low and take the seat at the head of the organization, but he knew he had to be careful about it. B-Low was well respected within his circle, and JP knew they would rise up for his cause. B-Low had more protection than the President, so the hit would have to be tactful and discreet; it was going to have to come from the inside. JP continued to pace the room, trying to think of a fool-proof way to get rid of B-Low.

Chapter 5

*B*efore Real could make it home, there were three missed calls on his cell phone from Cream. He thought about Constance, but had to put that thought behind him; he knew Cream was in the perfect position to help him get back to the top. Real pressed redial on his cell.

Cream picked up on the first ring. "Hey," she whispered as she headed to the bathroom, away from Dan.

"What up, baby girl?" Real asked, turning into the parking lot at his apartment complex.

"Nothing. Just thinkin' about you. Are you gonna be busy tomorrow?" Cream asked, still whispering.

"Nah, slow day tomorrow. What you got in mind?" Real asked, already knowing where Cream was headed with the conversation.

"Dan is going out of town tomorrow. How about you come over?" Cream asked suggestively.

"Let's eat at the Westin around 9:00," Real told her, sticking to his rules of never playing around with another man's lady in that man's home.

"Oh, okay. That's cool. We can… Yes, baby!" Cream called out to Dan, then flushed the toilet. "Be right out!"

"So 9:00?" Real repeated as he listened to her fumble around, trying to play it off.

"Yeah. See you then. Bye," Cream whispered, then quickly hung up the phone.

Real spent five more minutes just sitting in the car in front of his apartment, pondering the best approach to get the money needed to put the wheels back in motion.

Just as Real was exiting the car, someone in a black ski mask came out of nowhere. "Nigga, give it up!" the man demanded, shoving his gun into Real's back.

"Hold up, young blood. Ain't no need to pull that trigger. You can have everything I got. Ain't no buck in me, bro," Real said calmly as the man started going into Real's pockets.

Real looked down and noticed a tattoo on the man's hand.

After searching Real's pockets and coming up with a couple hundred dollars, the masked man slammed the butt of the gun into the back of Real's head, and then struck out running.

"Shit!!!" Real screamed, grabbing the back of his head and feeling a knot rising. "Fuck!" Real spat, massaging his head. He cursed under his breath all the way up to the door. He also made a mental note to add the nigga with "Jazz" tattooed across the back of his hand to the list of niggas he had to kill.

Real hurried into his apartment and poured himself a

stiff drink. As much as he knew a nice, fat line of coke could soothe his pain physically and mentally, Real refused and stuck to his decision to leave the drugs alone. Real knew he had to kick the habit soon; in just a matter of days, he'd have his hands on enough cocaine to supply a city—a big city at that.

Chapter 6

*J*P's sixth set of pull-ups was interrupted when his cell phone rang. "Yeah? What up?" he asked, with a hint of irritation in his voice.

"Say, JP, it's imperative that we meet up today. Meet me at my lot around noon," Seth ordered as he pushed his custom Audi R8 through the early-morning downtown traffic, en route to his exotic car lot in Buckhead, home to Atlanta's wealthiest.

"Okay, cool. Is everything a'ight?" JP asked, picking up on the seriousness in Seth's tone.

"We need to speed up the process. I'll fill you in when we meet," Seth said and then ended the call.

JP laid his cell phone on the weight bench, thought for a minute, then flexed in the floor-to-ceiling mirror, admiring the results of his early-morning workout. Just when he was about to knock out five more sets of crunches, his phone beeped again. "Hello?" he answered, slightly annoyed at the interruption.

"Yo, J, what's the biz? I need you to drive the van today. We got a big drop coming around 3:00, and you know I ain't trustin' nobody but you to handle it. I know we silenced Casey, but I got a gut feeling it's somebody else on the team who's playing two sides. Until we find the rat, we gotta handle all the drop-offs and pick-ups ourselves. Ya feel me?" B-Low told him as he counted the money for the drop and stacked the bills in $5,000 sets.

"That's cool, bro, but it's important that we find out who's putting shit in the game and get rid of them. They stopping the movement from running smooth. Who you got in mind, bro?" JP asked; he smiled, knowing the person in question was none other than himself.

"I been thinking...Troop, Veno, Celia, or Swag. Hmm, man. I can't put my finger on it. I'm just gonna give it time to show itself, because it will eventually come to light. I don't wanna jump the gun, man. Shit, I just can't call it right now for sure," B-Low said as he pushed the stacks of counted money to the side to make room for the uncounted.

"You right. Shit will surface, and when it do, I want to handle it personally. What time is the drop?" JP asked as he wiped the sweat from his brow and exited the gym.

"I need you at my spot at 3:00, and then we can meet Juan's lady friend around 4:00 and drop the money. The van'll be waiting for you at the Walmart across the street from the mall. Just park it in the garage at the stash house in Riverdale. We'll unload it later," B-Low told him as he steadily pulled money from a duffle bag and placed it on the table to be counted.

"A'ight. I'll be there. I'll holla," JP said

When he entered his bedroom, he saw Angela lying naked on top of the covers, lightly snoring, still tired from the long night of wild fucking.

Smack!

Angela's bottom wiggled and jiggled out of control. JP went to slap it a second time, but he paused when Angela quickly turned over and looked up at him. "Nigga!" she yelled, then threw a pillow at a fleeing JP. She'd been hanging around JP a lot lately, especially after eavesdropping on his telephone call. She really wanted a piece of the pie, and she was willing to put in some work to get it. She'd already formulated the perfect plan, and she would be the main player, because she knew B-Low's weakness for pussy. All she had to do was get JP to let her play the part, for a reasonable fee, of course. If he didn't cooperate, she would sell the information she knew to B-Low. Either way, from either man, she was gonna make a profit.

G STREET CHRONICLES
A NEW URBAN DYNASTY

WWW.GSTREETCHRONICLES.COM

Chapter 7

"*I* got a boatload of this shit arriving next week, and this ignorant nigger is testing my nerves!" Seth yelled to Jody, his right-hand man, as he sat in the back office of his exotic car lot.

"We really need B-Low out of the way if we're gonna meet our quota on time. That nigga's fucking up the game with them low prices of his. All our people are switching over and buying from his people. If we cut off his line, we'll be making five times more, and the product will move a whole lot faster. That will mean bigger profits on our end," Jody explained, looking out the office window at the brand new Rolls-Royce Phantom that had just arrived.

"I'm gonna give that nigger two days to get rid of our problem. If he don't, I'ma contact Vega to have him eliminate B-Low, the crew, *and* JP's sorry ass. JP knows too much to be walking around without being involved, so he'll most definitely need to be added to the list. On the other hand, if he handles the business at hand, we'll give him the West Coast to run. I know he'll be able to deal with the thugs real well out there," Seth said, rising out of his seat to look at the Phantom too.

"You sure you don't wanna contact Vega now? We need all this shit handled without hassle, as promptly as possible," Jody suggested as he turned and walked to the back of the office.

"Nah. I'm gonna give him till this weekend. If the job's not taken care of by then, I'll call Vega in to handle it," Seth said firmly.

Even though Jody was Seth's right-hand man, he wasn't always informed of Seth's moves, such as the two previous unsuccessful attempts to take out B-Low. Seth had come to the conclusion that B-Low was either extremely lucky or just untouchable. Two of the best in the business had been sent his way. The first one slipped on the kill, and a shootout ensued, leaving B-Low wounded and the hit man dead. The second attempt had been stopped by B-Low's private security; they all specialized in martial arts, and they'd damn near killed Ceaser, one of the best killers around. After those failed attempts, Seth realized the hit would have to come from within the organization, so he'd sought JP out and offered him wealth and a deal nobody in their right mind would refuse. At a dinner meeting set up by Seth and one of JP's mutual buyers, Seth had put his proposition on the table. It was a big risk: If JP had refused, it could have meant an all-out war, alerting B-Low of Seth's intentions in the process. So, Seth made sure to put a man in place to take care of JP if he refused.

The proposition that was put in front of JP was one that would change his life and make him very wealthy. He knew Seth's power extended around the world, and he wasn't about to pass up a chance to be a part of the movement. Besides that, the crumbs B-Low was paying him were nowhere near what he thought he deserved. To live the high life and be in control of his own territory, he had to get rid of B-Low. It would be no easy task, but JP wanted in, so he agreed.

"Okay. Just give me the word, but don't procrastinate too long, because the product will be arriving soon. Damn B-Low's still got a stronghold on some prime territories," Jody said as he exited the office.

"Don't worry. Low's time is limited," Seth hollered to Jody, grabbing a bag of pretzels off his desk. He started crunching on them as he walked back to the window to admire the Rolls-Royce again.

Jody stuck his head back in the office door. "If you need me, I'll be in the garage," then headed out there to make sure the pick-up car was ready to go.

Seth walked back over to his desk and looked over some paperwork while he waited for JP to arrive.

At a quarter past 12:00, JP pulled into the car dealership. His Lexus looked like a cheap Toyota compared to all the more expensive cars on the lot. As JP walked up to the office door, he pictured himself sitting behind the wheel of one of the many quarter-million-dollar automobiles that surrounded him.

Seth saw him approaching and stepped outside his office door to wave him in. "Hey, JP. What's going on, buddy? It's good to see you again," Seth said insincerely as he extended his hand to JP.

"Ain't shit happening. Business as usual, buddy," JP said sarcastically. Deep down, he hated and wanted to kill the arrogant Jew who sat across from him, but he knew he wouldn't live to see the next day if he even tried. JP was very familiar with Seth and his entourage, and he knew Seth was a very dangerous man. The people who backed him were very loyal to him—not to mention ten times more dangerous. Besides that, Seth was his ticket to the top.

"Have a seat. You like that one?" Seth asked, noticing JP admiring the half-million-dollar Phantom glistening in the sunlight.

"Yeah, that bitch hard," JP replied as he took a seat on the plush leather office couch that sat against the far wall of Seth's expensively furnished office.

"Yeah, the car is hard, but it's not hard to get if you're in the right position," Seth stated, sitting behind his office desk in his oversized winged leather chair.

"Position. It's all about position," JP mumbled, taking another lustful glance at the car.

"Yeah, you got that right," Seth agreed.

"So, what's the deal? Surely you didn't call me all the way out here to talk about a new Rolls. Is there some kind of problem?" JP asked, leaning up on the couch.

"Yeah, there is a problem. It's B-Low. We can't put it off any longer. We've gotta get rid of this little problem now. He's getting in the way, and he's gotta be taken care of by the weekend, no ifs, ands, or buts about it," Seth said firmly, glaring across his cherry-oak desk at JP.

"By the weekend? Man, that's impossible with all the secur—"

"By the weekend," Seth repeated sternly and cutting off JP's excuses. "And by the way, how's life treating you?" he asked, changing the subject.

"I'll be in touch," JP spat as he stood. He walked to the door to leave, though what he really wanted to do was jump behind the desk and ram his 9mm in Seth's mouth.

"Okay, buddy. I look forward to hearing from you soon," Seth replied, wearing a firm, serious look on his face that quickly curled into a sinister smile.

As JP exited, he wondered why the powerful and dangerous Seth didn't just go ahead and have someone else eliminate B-Low. He wanted to figure that out, but he dismissed the thought with a shrug as he climbed behind the wheel of his Lexus. On his way to take care of the shipment, he mentally played out several ways to take B-Low out.

As soon as JP exited the office, Seth picked up the phone and called Jody out in the detail shop. "Jody, put Vega on standby. There's been a change of plans," Seth said, not at all comfortable with the way his meeting with JP has gone.

"I'll give him all the info on B-Low and tell him to wait for me to give the word," Jody said on the other end, smiling and glad to hear that their competition was about to be eliminated.

"No, put him on standby to take care of JP after he handles B-Low for us," Seth said, grabbing another handful of pretzels.

"Oh. Okay, I' on it," Jody replied without question.

Chapter 8

*A*s Real headed out the door en route to the Westin to meet Cream, his cell phone buzzed. "Yeah?" Real answered, trying to talk over the clunking motor of the old Buick he was driving.

"Real, I got a problem. I can't find my keys anywhere. Are you at the hotel yet?" Cream asked as she frantically tore up the house, looking for her keys.

"Nah. I'm on my way though," Real answered, then paused, waiting for her response.

"Can you come by and pick me up?" she asked, giving up on her search.

"Cream, man, you sure you can't find your keys?"

"I've looked everywhere."

"Where you stayin'?" Real asked reluctantly, still not wanting to step in another man's territory.

"I'm out in Alpharetta. If you can come get me, I'll have my girlfriend to pick me up from the room," Cream pleaded. Cream had been after Real every since he'd opened up the G-Spot years earlier. She was pretty sure that his only hang-up had been his girl Constance, and she wasn't in the picture anymore. Cream wasn't about to let her chance at spending a night with Real get away, even if she had to walk to the hotel in her fancy heels.

"A'ight, I'll come snatch you up, but look…I ain't taking you back," Real told her firmly. He listened to her directions to her spot, then whipped the Buick around and headed back north to Alpharetta.

He pushed the Buick fast as he could, but it wouldn't get up over sixty MPH for some reason. As he drove, he thought of the best way to get Cream to help fund his come-up. Real knew Dan, the rich old white man, was the key.

He exited off the expressway and made a left, following Cream's directions. Just as he turned left onto Kilgor Road, the junky old Buick spat a big cloud of black smoke, jerked for a quarter-mile, then died right in front of a church.

"Fuck! Fuck!" Real shouted as he pushed the car door open and stepped out in the middle of the deserted back street. After looking at the car and determining it was a useless hunk of metal, he pulled his cell from his pocket and dialed Cream's number.

"You almost here?" Cream asked as soon as she answered.

"Man, my shit done broke down on me in front of some goddamn church. Fuck!" Real said, disgusted as he looked down the dark road.

"What? A church? Where?" Cream asked, pacing the

room in her Chanel ensemble.

"It's, uh, St. John's Methodist, on, uh—"

"Kilgor Road?"

"Yeah."

"You're right around the corner from my house. Do you see the street next to the church?"

"Yeah."

"I stay on that street, second house on the left," Cream said, glad to hear he was right around the corner.

"A'ight. I'm on my way. Keep trying to find those keys," Real said. He left the Buick on the side if the road and started walking.

Turning the corner at the church, he saw a row of beautiful mansions that had to be listed at a million or more each. He looked up the hill to the left and found the address he was looking for. When he saw Cream's digs, he had to do a double take. The house was huge, with a brightly lit fountain out in front of it. Real was more than impressed; the place even put his old crib—the one he'd had when he was *the* man—to shame. He knew Dan was stacking paper, but he'd never imagined the man was that loaded. He hated going against his rule of never stepping in another man's spot, but he had to make an exception; thanks to his piece-of-shit car, it was his only choice. He wasn't worried so much since Dan was out of town—not to mention he had his old .38 tucked away in the waistband of his slacks.

Walking up the driveway to the immaculate home, Real felt bad, reflecting on how good he once had it. Seeing that mansion really motivated him to get back to the good life he'd once lived. Before he could knock Cream greeted him at the door. She was dressed in a form-fitting red dress that accentuated all her fine curves, and Real couldn't help staring at her wide hips and perfect C-cups; she was perfect in his eyes.

"Hey, baby! Come on in," she said excitedly, stepping aside for Real to enter.

As Real entered the mansion, he was hit with a slight wave of jealousy. The house was professionally decorated, equipped with some of the sleekest electronics on the market. Real was highly impressed with the pearly marble floors in the foyer and the white grand piano that sat in the dayroom in front of the floor-to-ceiling picture window.

"Oh, Real, it's so good to see you!" Cream said as she walked up and wrapped her arms around him tightly.

A feeling of guilt ran through Real as he thought about Constance. He remembered the many occasions when she'd complained about Cream coming on to him, and now there he was, standing in the woman's place, with her all hugging up on him. "Hey, baby. It's good to see you too. Damn, it's been a minute. Where's your old man at?" Real asked, still hating going against one of his number one rules.

"Don't trip over him, Real. Dan's gonna be gone for a whole week. He's out in L.A. on some business. What's up with your car?" Cream asked, loosening her embrace and leading him over to the den, where a seventy-two-inch flat-screen covered the wall.

"The hell if I know. I need to find another ride," Real said as he walked over to the coffee table and looked at the pictures of Dan and Cream.

"I know my keys are here somewhere. I'll find them. Anyway, what's up with you, Mr. Real?" Cream said, shamelessly invading his personal space and grabbing his hand.

"Trying to make shit happen. I gotta get back to the top, where I belong, and I'm looking for the right woman to hold me down," Real said, pulling her close to him by the hips.

"Is that so? Where your little wifey Constance?" Cream asked jokingly as she reached up and hooked her arms around his neck.

The mention of Constance turned Real's stomach; he knew he was wrong for being in Cream's place, holding her in his arms. "Didn't work out. Uh...just didn't work," Real lied as Constance's beautiful face popped up in his head.

"Aw. I'm sorry to hear that. You two looked good together. How about a drink?" Constance suggested. Not waiting for an answer, she turned and headed to the bar. A couple minutes later, she returned with two glasses of Grey Goose, on the rocks. "Here. Drink this. Vodka's good for the nerves. Do you think you can fix your car? If you can do it yourself, Dan's got every damn tool in the world."

"Yeah, I gotta try something. Where the tools at?" Real asked as he took a large gulp of Grey Goose.

"In the garage, on the back wall. He got every tool known to man," Cream said, sipping on her drink and looking Real up and down like she wanted to be sipping on him instead.

"Lemme check his hardware out," Real told Cream as he got up and made his way to the side door that he figured would lead to the garage.

"Okay. I'll go freshen up while you look!" Cream called out as she hurried upstairs to slip into something a lot more comfortable since it appeared their evening plans had changed and they wouldn't be going out for a while, if at all.

Real checked out all the expensive paintings as he made his way to the garage. When he opened the garage door, he stepped in and instantly became excited. The two Ducati sports bikes that sat before him were his favorites. He went over to get a closer look at them and couldn't resist the urge to throw his leg over the seat of one. He pulled the bike to him to size it up. *Man, I can't wait to get back to the top of the game,* he thought. Enjoying grown men's toys again would make it all worthwhile.

He finally got off the bike and looked over at the five-foot toolbox up against the back corner wall. As he walked toward it, he thought about his plan to seduce the hell out of Cream so he could convince her to dig deep into Dan's pocket to finance his start-up. When he reached the toolbox, he pulled out the bottom drawer. He didn't see anything that would assist him in fixing his trashy Buick back to running condition. The middle drawer wouldn't open easily, so he had to pull it open with all his might. When he finally jerked it hard enough, it snapped opened. Much to Real's surprise, he found himself looking down on at least a dozen nice, high-powered handguns. With his curiosity piqued, he opened each drawer, finding more weapons in each one. The top drawer was the only exception: It held stacks of cash wrapped in plastic. Real smiled and wasted no time in pulling the money from the drawer.

Five minutes later, Cream walked in. "What's taking so… Real, baby, what are you doing?" Cream asked, surprised and angry at herself for unknowingly sending Real to the place where Dan kept his stash.

"I want you on my team, Cream. You know how I roll. This crack ain't talking 'bout shit you ne—"

"No, Real! I ain't gonna do it like this. Dan will have the both of us killed! Real, if you take that money, you're doing us both in!" Cream snapped, hoping Real would reconsider.

As she protested, Real knew the only one he had to worry about was himself. No one but him and Cream knew what he was up to, and seeing how she was acting, he knew if it came down to it, she'd give him up. It was a risk he couldn't take, and his resurrection to power and prestige meant more to him than she did.

Chapter 9

B-Low sat there, waiting on JP to show so they could handle the drop. Funny things had been going on inside the organization, and something still just wasn't sitting right with B-Low. He'd dealt with Casey, but he still felt like somebody else in the circle wasn't right. He ran the members' names through his head: *Grump? Naw. Kap? Nope. Yella? Nikki? No way.* He didn't even bother naming JP because he knew it wasn't him. Twenty minutes later, he was still lost in thought when JP pulled up outside his mini mansion that sat on acres and acres of well-manicured land in Fayetteville, Georgia.

JP got angry every time he pulled up on B-Low's spot. He felt he deserved to be living the same way, but he was stuck with a modest quarter-mill, two-bedroom spot that looked like a shack compared to B-Low's accommodations. If it wasn't for JP himself, B-Low wouldn't have been living such a life of luxury. Slamming the car into park, he got out and briskly walked up to the door. JP never revealed his dislike or jealousy, because he knew it would arouse suspicion and spoil his takeover.

Knock! Knock!

Minutes later, B-Low opened the door so JP could enter.

JP's heart raced as he walked through the house. The 500-gallon fish tank was the focal point in the foyer. Off to the side, against the wall, were some very rare African artifacts and other rare collectibles.

They entered B-Low's home library to wait for the call to move out.

"Yo, look, bro. Somebody in the circle still ain't right. I just checked on my drop, and word is that the nigga Seth is trying to knock my hustle. That bitch-ass half-breed knows how much I'm paying for my drop. He knows when it's scheduled to drop and how many I'm buyin', even though only the people in our circle are supposed to know all that shit. He got too much info. He fucking keep on getting the up on me with the buyers. The fucker's undercutting me bad, and he's really gotta be making peanuts at the rate he's going. Anyway, bro, we got a rat in the house, so it's time to set a rat trap," B-Low said firmly as he paced the floor.

"Seth? Man, that nigga still around? Last I heard, he'd moved his operation up to NY. But yeah, if we got a rat, we need to set a damn trap," JP spat, thinking about the consequences that would befall him if B-Low found out he was the one behind it all.

"Let's ride," B-Low called out after getting a text from the man in charge of Juan's drop-offs.

Before they reached the front door, Blu and Quad moved in, positioning themselves in front and back of B-Low. JP was moved out of the circle they made as they exited the house. B-Low kept tight security around him at all times, especially since the last failed attempt on his life. He'd once been a street gangsta, a straight-up killer who'd mocked any nigga who used bodyguards, but now he relied on his. Blu and Quad, like most of his security, were martial arts experts, and they were also licensed to carry firearms. They made it their business daily to protect the man who paid them so well.

JP jumped in his Lexus, while Quad and Blu ushered B-Low over to his F-250. After securing B-Low, the goons fell back and got in their Crown Vic and followed B-Low's every turn.

When he pulled up into the Walmart parking lot, JP saw the van with the shipment, parked off to the side.

Simultaneously, on the other side of town, B-Low met with Juan's girl to drop off the money. As soon as the bag of cash was in her hand, she pulled out her cell and texted someone. That person then walked out of Walmart and dropped the van keys in the window.

Watching from afar, JP knew everything was a go. He entered the van, grabbed the keys off the floorboard, and cranked the engine. Then he drove off toward the stash house, where he would pull it in the garage and leave it for B-Low to count and prepare for distribution. He called B-Low as he exited the lot. "Shit straight. Headed to the stash spot," JP said, though he was entertaining the thought of taking off with the whole shipment himself.

"A'ight. Just holla at me tomorrow so we can put this shit in the streets," B-Low said, headed back to his spot with Quad and Blu trailing close behind him.

"Okay. I'll holla," JP responded, knowing that he would have to wait at the stash house for his ride back to the Walmart to get his car.

As soon as his ride back to Walmart arrived, an unmarked official car pulled up, paused, then pulled off. The federal agent knew to be discreet while they built a solid case for Operation Down Low.

Chapter 10

"Real, I can't let you just take his money. Please don't," Cream begged as she walked up on Real while he continued unloading the money and guns from the toolbox.

"You coming or what?" Real asked, trying his best to get Cream to agree so he could spare her.

"No!" Cream said. She turned and stomped back into the house. She was in such a huff that she wasn't even aware Real was following close behind her.

By the time she got to the phone, Real had the .38 out and was ready to let loose. "Put it down!" Real screamed, startling her.

She dropped the phone and looked back at him. "Real, baby, please don't do this!" Cream begged as she walked over to him and dropped down in front of him, crying.

Real hadn't had a conscience since his baby girl had been killed, so Cream's pleading went unnoticed. He thought it over for only a second before he knew what had to be done.

Pop!

Cream had her head down in her hands, crying hysterically, when the .38 bullet pierced the top of her head.

Pop!

The second shot sealed the deal. Real hated that it had come to that, but she was his only link to the scene. Turning and walking off, he cursed under his breath.

Back in the garage, he made sure to wipe the place clean of fingerprints. He made sure he didn't touch anything else while he loaded the money up in a hunting bag he found sitting next to the toolbox. After loading up, he used an old towel to open the garage door so he wouldn't leave his prints behind. He then jumped on one of the old man's Ducatis. The engine came to life instantly. He positioned the helmet on his head, threw the bike into first gear, and took off.

Real rode the stolen motorcycle fast and hard, thinking about what was about to come. He had over a quarter-million in cash and over $100,000 worth of guns. Calculating the take, he knew he had enough to jump-start his reign of terror. He planned to get in touch with Kimono, the same man he planned to step on while making his way back to the top.

An hour later, Real was sitting in his shabby apartment, sorting through the guns. He chose a couple for his own personal use, then bagged the others up to sell.

Later, as he was lying in bed, Real talked to Constance as if she was right there next to him. *Don't worry, baby. As soon as I get myself situated back on top, I'm gonna see Cash, B-Low, and the Italians for the grief they brought on our once-perfect lives.*

Chapter 11

*J*P walked through the door with a lot on his mind, and it showed.

Angela noticed the worried look as he entered the bedroom and sat down on the side of the bed. She hoped he hadn't made a move on B-Low without her. "Baby, what's wrong?" she asked as she slid over and sat beside him.

"Nothing. Ain't shit. I'm cool," he said, with a hint of irritation in his tone.

"You look like you stressing. Lie back and let Mama take care of you," Angela said, moving closer and pulling up his shirt.

"Not right now, baby," JP blurted out and rose up off the bed.

Angela had planned to fuck and suck her way into the play on B-Low, but since JP wasn't in the mood, she decided to just come straight out with it. "Let me help you get B-Low," she said firmly as she got up and walked over to him.

"What?" JP questioned. *Did she really just say that?*

"Look, JP…straight up, I heard you on the phone the other day, talking about taking B-Low out. Let me make some money on this shit," Angela demanded.

JP was totally caught off guard by her statement and, more so, by the fact that she wanted to be part of it. Knowing that time was running out and that B-Low was hard to get to, he quickly factored in how she might be of help. "So you know, huh? What you want out of the deal, Angela?" JP asked, upset that Angela knew his business. He realized she could be a catalyst to his death with that information, but then again, she could also turn out to be a real asset if he worked it right.

"Just set me up nicely out in Atlantic Station and put $200,000 in the bank for me," Angela said firmly. She knew she had the upper hand in the situation with the information she now possessed.

"Did you say 200 bands? Come on, now. For that, you gotta pull the trigger on the nigga your-damn-self!" JP spat, not liking the numbers Angela was requesting.

"I'll pull the trigger if you add $50,000 more. You can just sit back and get ready to take over the organization while I eliminate this little problem of yours," Angela said with conviction in her voice.

JP thought about her proposition and mentally added up the money he had stashed. He knew if he paid her $250,000, he'd be taking quite a hit, but he also knew he'd get that back and a whole lot more if he was given his own territory to run. "A'ight," he finally answered.

"You got it, but it's gotta be done before the weekend," JP declared as he walked over and peeked out the window after hearing a car out front.

"Okay. I got you, but I need half up front," Angela said with confidence.

"Fine. Just let me know where you want it to go," JP replied, stepping to the window to look out again.

"I'll text you with the info," Angela said before she got up and started getting dressed.

"So you out, just like that?" JP asked, sounding disappointed. He was suddenly in the mood again, and he wanted to get his rocks off with a quickie.

"I got work to do, baby. I'll be back tomorrow," she said as she grabbed her keys and turned to leave.

"A'ight then. Lock the door behind you," JP told her as she exited.

JP went over the agreement he'd made with her, and he really did feel good about it. In time, he would be on top, with his own organization, and the thought of that made him smile. He peeked out the window and watched Angela pull off, but he failed to notice the black Yukon following her, with two federal agents hidden well behind its tinted windows.

Chapter 12

The next day, Real was up early. He made a couple calls, then made his way out to see Kimono, the biggest heroin dealer in the South. Real had decided against cocaine; he saw a quicker come-up in dealing with the boy.

He knew he'd have to dump the stolen Ducati soon, so he made plans to grab a ride. Hitting the back roads on the Ducati had Real's adrenaline pumping. He loved the raw power of the bike rumbling beneath him. In no time he was out front of the deli where Kimono did business in Clayton County. He parked the bike and hopped off with the bag of money secured in a pack on his back.

As soon as he hit the door, Kimono waved him over and around to the back. There was no one but an old man cutting meat in the spot. Real followed Kimono to the back, knowing the whole time that if he was going to take over, Kimono, too, would have to be eliminated; Kimono had no idea his days were numbered.

"Yo, Real! Long time no see," said Kimono, the

unsuspecting half-black, half-Japanese man as he led Real to a back room to handle the business at hand.

Kimono and Real had been running in the same circle for years, but they'd never done business with each other since one dealt in cocaine and the other in heroin. Now that Real had made the switch, he and Kimono had been brought together through a mutual friend.

"Yeah, I been busy. I see you're still doing your thang," Real told him, glancing at the photographs of all the famous people who frequented the popular deli.

"Yeah, I'm hanging. What you spending?" Kimono asked as he pulled a metal folding chair out of the office closet and positioned it beside his desk for his guest.

"I'm looking at $150,000. What can you do for that?" Real asked.

Kimono instantly started running figures through his head. "I will fuck with you for ten since it's you," Kimono said, wearing a sly smile.

"Run it. Here ya go," Real said. He pulled the pack off and handed the money to Kimono.

"Gimme a couple minutes," Kimono told Real as he pulled out his cell to make a call. Minutes later, he was giving Real directions to the pick up spot.

"Appreciate ya. I'll be in touch," Real said, looking down at the strip of paper with the address on it.

After picking up his package, Real hit the streets, putting the word out. All his old connects with heroin customers jumped right back onboard. He stopped at all the dope spots and let it be known that he was back and that he wasn't taking no shorts. By later in the evening,

Real's phone was chirping with orders from all over the city. Real knew then that he'd have the whole city again soon. *It's just a matter of time.*

* * *

That same day, Kimono called his cartel connect and set up a special order because he'd sold more than he'd expected to. "Yo, Carlo, I need more product. Things are looking up for me out here. Maybe I'll soon be as rich as you," he said playfully as he counted the money up for his next buy.

"Damn, man! You moving big weight, I see," Carlo joked.

"Yeah, that boy Real, who used to own that club G Spot, is back in town. He only wants the heroin now. I can tell by his digs that he's been out of the loop for a minute. I guess he's trying to make a comeback, this time with a different product," Kimono said, placing the cash in a brown bag.

"Real? You say he's been out of the loop. Has this guy been to prison?" Carlo asked as he lounged out by his pool.

"Yeah, I think so. He never really came out and said it, but I could see it all over his face. I figure that's why I haven't seen him around lately," Kimono declared as he tucked the bag of money between the trash bags that sat next to the door.

"Hmm. Is he tall, with dark skin and crazy eyes?" Carlo asked, surprised by what he was hearing. He remembered hearing that Real was supposed to be dead.

"Yeah, that's him. You know Real?" Kimono asked, trying to make the connection.

"Yeah, he's an old friend. You know where he lays his head?" Carlo asked with concern in his voice, knowing Real might be a potential threat to the family.

"Nah, but I can find out," Kimono replied, hoping to get in with the man who was part of one of the strongest cartels in the States and abroad.

"No, I'll find out for myself. What was he driving, and how long ago did he leave?" Carlo asked, thinking of his police connect in Atlanta.

"Not too long ago. He was on a motorcycle, some nice red and gray bike," Kimono told him, trying to get some brownie points with the man.

"Thanks," Carlo said and ended the call.

Seconds later, Carlo was on the phone with his police connect. Not long after relaying the information, a police car was dispatched through a private line used only for such occasions. Sergeant West called Jacobs, the uniformed officer who was on his payroll, and relayed the information.

Jacobs loved when his private line beeped because he knew that meant some extra money was about to come his way. He knew not to arrest the person in question; he was only supposed to pull him over and get all the information he could. Luck was on his side, for he was already in the vicinity of the man on the red and gray motorcycle.

Chapter 13

*R*eal made sure he stayed within the speed limit while pushing the bike out to Memorial Drive to meet up with an old connect who might be able to help him find a ride. As he neared the 285 entrance ramp, he noticed a police car rushing in his direction. Staying calm, he made sure he didn't violate any traffic laws as he came up to the turn to merge onto the highway. Real knew the bike hadn't been reported stolen as of yet since Cream was dead and Dan was still in LA, so he didn't panic.

Just as he was about to make the turn onto the highway, the police car lights lit up, and the officer signaled for Real to pull the bike over. Jacobs hoped the man on the bike was the person of interest so he could report his findings and get paid. Jacobs pulled behind the bike and cautiously stepped out and motioned for the biker to get off the motorcycle. He got within a couple of feet of the bike before it roared to life.

Real had second thoughts. *Maybe someone came*

home, found Cream, and reported the damn bike stolen. Shit! He couldn't take any chances, and he wasn't about to go back to prison. Seconds before the police officer got within an arm's reach of him, the bike was propelling its way onto 285, blending in with the evening traffic.

"Shit!" Jacobs spat as he turned and ran back to his patrol car to give chase, glad that the Atlanta PD had upgraded his car to the new Mustang 5.0, which had enough punch to at least keep the bike in sight.

Real's trek on the bike didn't last long. By the time he got to the 285/85 connector, the bike was puttering down, out of fuel. Wanting to kick himself in the ass, he took the first exit in sight, hoping to find a gas station.

Jacobs saw the bike slowing up ahead, exiting the expressway. He stepped on the gas, and it didn't take long for him to catch up with the bike. He could tell the man on the bike wanted to get off it and take off running, but it would have been no use since the exit ramp was flanked with marsh and heavy bush. His prey was stuck.

Real was pissed. He twisted the throttle again and again, hoping the bike would sputter back to life to get him far enough away from the cop, but it wouldn't cooperate. He looked back and saw the police car, well out of its district, coming at him full speed ahead.

Minutes later, the tall, lanky, white officer was jumping out of the car, commanding Real to get down while pointing his state-issued Glock at him.

Real knew there was no use trying to run because he wouldn't get far on foot in that unmaintained terrain, so he stepped away from the bike with his hands up.

Spectators had their cell phones out, catching video and just being nosy.

Jacobs knew he had to move fast to take care of his dirty-cop business before a fellow officer came to render aid. "Get down now!" Jacobs screamed, angry that he had to actually work for his money.

"Just calm down, man. I'm gettin' down," Real told Jacobs as he dropped to his knees on the side of the off ramp.

Jacobs knew he would be on permanent desk duty if another officer or anyone in the department reported his actions. He had to move fast. "Give me you driver's license and insurance for this bike, and explain to me why you're running!" Jacobs demanded, standing over Real.

Real carefully dug in his back pocket to retrieve his wallet.

Jacobs didn't wait for him to remove his ID. Instead, he just snatched the wallet from Real and started going through it. He looked carefully at the contents and memorized the address he saw: *3125 Club Candlewood Drive, Apartment 36, East Point, Georgia. Got it.* Satisfied, he tossed Real's wallet and its contents next to him on the ground.

Real was speechless, still on his knees with his hands behind his head with cards and documents strewn all over the ground around him.

"It's your lucky day," Jacobs spat as he turned and walked back to his running patrol car.

Real didn't understand the officer's strange actions, but he didn't waste time trying to figure them out either.

He took a deep breath as he watched the officer speed by him to exit the highway. Once the police Mustang was out of sight, he got up and walked off the exit.

He called his connect about a car, and the guy met him thirty minutes later with something to ride in. Real was quite happy with the Dodge Ram, black, with dark-tinted windows. It would be just right for scouting the streets unseen, looking for some old acquaintances who were on deck for payback.

Chapter 14

The next day, all the heads of the cartel families met at Angelo's Miami home. They all took their seats in the lavishly furnished library in the west wing of the multimillion-dollar estate.

"Gentlemen, I called this meeting because I got word last night that Real—the man who killed two of our beloved heads last year—is still alive, even though we were told he'd been taken care of. He is out of prison, alive and well, back in Atlanta," Carlo announced with a look of disdain and worry on his face as he looked at each member of the cartel that sat before him.

"That can't be! Real is dead. The money for the hit was deposited a year ago. Where did you get this information from? Who are your sources?" Angelo asked Carlo in disbelief. He looked over at Michael, who now controlled the Cadoza family; Michael had assured the families that Real was dead and wouldn't be a threat anymore.

"Your sources, whoever they are, are wrong, Carlo.

I took care of Real's elimination myself. I'm more than sure that the man is dead. My prison connect assured me that the little bastard had been taken care of, " Michael blurted out nervously, hoping he'd been told the truth. He made a mental note to call the chaplain; he hadn't heard from the man since the day he'd wired the money for the hit.

"Sorry, Michael, but Real is very much alive, staying in Club Candlewood apartments out on the south side of Atlanta, Apartment 36, to be exact," Carlo emphasized to the men, making sure to magnify Michael's incompetence.

"Can this information be true, Michael?" Milo asked angrily, pissed at Michael's mishandling of what should have been a simple behind-bars hit.

"I'm 99 percent sure. I saw to it personally!" Michael spat heatedly as he pushed his chair back from the table and stood.

Angelo leaned back in his seat, looked over angrily at Michael, and then spoke. "Carlo, get with your sources and double check this. I need to know every detail. If it's true that Real is still alive, I want him dead…and this time, I want his body brought to me personally," Angelo ordered as he pondered what Michael's punishment should be. He was now the head of one of the cartel's most powerful families, so any plans to dispose of Michael would have to be brought before the board. He was sure the vote would not be in favor of punishing Michael for his accidental dishonesty.

On the other hand, hot-headed Milo didn't care what the other bosses had to say about it. He was going to punish Michael for not taking care of Real like he was supposed to.

"That's all for today, gentlemen. Thanks for taking time out of your busy schedules on such short notice to discuss this with me. I felt everyone should be aware of this man just in case he tries to strike again," Carlo announced.

The other men in attendance whispered amongst themselves as they all rose to leave.

Chapter 15

" *H*ey, B-Low, are you busy?" Angela asked B-Low after making sure JP had deposited half of her $250,000 like they had agreed. She'd also made sure he'd put a deposit on her spot out in Atlantic Station.

"Hey, baby. What up? What you been up to, girl?" B-Low said with enthusiasm as he sat in his TV room watching *SportsCenter.*

"Just trying to make it…and thinking about you. Why haven't you called me?" Angela asked in her baby voice as she looked down at the gun and silencer JP had given her to make the kill.

"Things been crazy. Anyway, I thought you and JP was doing y'all thang," B-Low replied, rubbing his growing hard-on as he thought back on all the good sex he'd enjoyed with Angela underneath him, in front of him, on top of him, and every which way.

"JP? Oh, that was way back when. I ain't talked to him in a minute. But anyway, what's up with you, boo? We kicking it tonight, or do you got another woman to tend to?" Angela asked as she picked up the lightweight plastic Glock and looked at it from side to side.

B-Low knew Angela was a gold-digger: Nine times out of ten, she was after rent money or cash for some other bill she was behind on. But since he didn't have anything else lined up and had a couple hundred to spare, he agreed on a date. "Yeah, we can do that. How 'bout you come out to my spot? We can do the dinner-and-a-movie thang in my newly upgraded home theatre. You'll be the first to experience the new Bose surround-sound system," B-Low joked as he flipped the channel to *Love and Hip Hop.*

"Oh, I feel so special! But just so you know, I ain't trying to do the three- or four-way thang tonight," she spat, laying the gun back on the bathroom counter.

"Three-way thang? What you talking about, girl?" B-Low asked, completely lost.

"You know—me, you, and those two goons of yours," Angela called out with emphasis, making sure he picked up on her dislike of his bodyguards.

"Oh! Nah, don't worry, baby. Them niggas got other business, and it ain't like it used to be when I was warring. Now they only around when I go out. While I'm safe up in my crib, they know to fall back," B-Low explained.

Angela picked the gun back up and pointed it in the mirror, admiring her reflection with the powerful piece in her grasp. "Okay. What time should I be there?" Angela asked.

"'Bout 10:00. I'll be finished taking care of business

by then," B-Low said, fondly remembering that Angela always swallowed every last drop after each episode.

"See you then. Bye," Angela cooed as she hung up the phone and pointed the gun in the mirror again, wearing a satisfied smirk on her face.

Angela had already run her plan past JP, who'd signed off on it. She planned to kill B-Low in his own house. She would keep the gun tucked in her purse next to the handcuffs for the kinky sex she had planned for B-Low. Her whole plan centered on getting B-Low to let her handcuff him to the bed; that wouldn't be so hard since she planned to add a little something extra to his drink.

As the night progressed, Angela grew more and more nervous. At first it seemed simple, but the closer it got to the time for her to act on her part of the deal, the more scared she got. She was on her third shot of tequila when her phone rang. "Hello?" she answered, slightly feeling the effects of the alcohol.

"You good? We still on for tonight, right?" JP asked, making sure she hadn't had any second thoughts or gotten cold feet.

"Yeah, I'm good. I'm about to head out to go get with him. Just make sure you've got all my money when it's all said and done," she said, slurring mildly.

"I got you. Just make sure you handle your biz, and the money's yours," JP said firmly as he ended the call.

Angela looked at the clock: It was nearing 9:30, the time she had planned to pull out. She picked up her purse and pulled out the Glock to inspect it once more. Angela gripped the weapon tightly in her hand, closed her eyes, and second-guessed herself. In that moment, she realized she couldn't do it. She couldn't possibly pull the trigger on B-Low. But a few minutes later, thinking about all that money and her new place, she had regained her nerve and was on her way out to B-Low's spot trying her best to keep her nerves intact.

Twenty minutes later, she was pulling up at B-Low's beautiful mansion. She made sure the Glock was safe and secure before she stepped out of the car. Walking up to the door, she put on her game face.

Knock! Knock!

Seconds later, the door opened, and there B-Low stood in a wife-beater and basketball shorts.

"Hey, babyyyy!" Angela smiled as B-Low pulled her in and took her in his arms.

"What up, you sexy bitch?" B-Low said forcefully as he grinded on her and kissed her greedily. He was, in fact, crazy about Angela, but he liked her better as a fuck-buddy than a wife. He didn't understand why any dude would marry a stripper or porn star. In B-Low's world, women like that were only good for a good nut. Looking at Angela, he was past worked up, and he didn't waste any time in getting to the point. "Come here," he said, grabbing the back of her head as he closed the door behind her.

Angela was well aware of what he wanted, and she obliged, knowing she had to play the game all the way till she was in position. She knelt down, pulled his rock-hard dick from his pants, and started sucking.

"Oh yeah! Suck that dick, baby. Damn, it's...been a...

minute. Shit!" B-Low moaned.

Angela deep-throated him and caressed his scrotum while he fucked her mouth. "Mmm…you like?" she asked between sucks, looking up at him.

"Hell yeah. Shit! Oh…God, it's about to—" B-Low moaned, but he was cut off midsentence when Angela stopped sucking and pulled his manhood from her mouth.

"Don't cum yet, baby. I want you in me," Angela said softly as she stood erect and insisted that they find the bedroom.

"A'ight. Let's go." B-Low smiled as he grabbed her hand and led her through the house to his bedroom.

As Angela walked through the door, her eyes combed over the custom-made bed; there was no place for her to cuff him. She would have to find a different way to go through with her plan. "Get naked," she ordered as they both climbed into the bed.

"Straight to the point, I see," B-Low joked as he stripped down and climbed up under the covers.

"Let me pee first," Angela said. She grabbed her purse and headed to the bathroom. In the bathroom, she pulled the gun out. She took a deep breath, opened the bathroom door, and looked over at B-Low, who had his head tilted back and his eyes closed, waiting on her to return to the bed. Angela counted to three, then stepped out of the bathroom with gun in hand. She crept quietly up to the side of the bed, just close enough so she wouldn't miss, and then she aimed the gun and closed her eyes.

Beep! Beep!

B-Low's cell interrupted his wait, and he opened his

eyes reflexively. When he did, he saw Angela pointing the Glock at him. He rolled out of the bed just as she pulled the trigger.

Pop! Pop! Pop! She pulled the trigger three more times, unbelievingly missing her target.

B-Low had rolled off the side of the bed and found the .12-gauge he kept under the bed for just that kind of situation. When he pulled the trigger, the *Boom!* shook the room. *Kaboom!* B-Low fired again.

Angela dropped the pistol and turned to run.

"Naw, bitch! It's too late for runnin' now!" B-Low screamed as he leveled for another shot, but then he changed his mind and dropped the gun.

Angela's heart raced as she tried her best to get away. She knew she had fucked up, and now she was running for dear life.

"Bitch, naw!" B-Low screamed. He quickly caught up with her, grabbed her by the hair, and snatched her to him.

"Please, B-Low! I was forced to do it! Please!" Angela screamed.

B-Low slung her to the floor and sat on top of her. "Bitch, you tried to kill me! You no-good, fuck-ass ho! Bitch, you 'bout to die!" B-Low said in a menacing tone. *Smack! Smack! Smack!* B-Low slapped Angela and didn't stop until he saw blood.

"Please no! JP made me do it!" Angela cried.

The mention of JP's name made B-Low freeze in his tracks. "JP?" B-Low called out, stunned by the accusation.

"Yes, he made me do it! He said if I didn't kill you, he'd kill me!" Angela lied to save her own life, crying hysterically.

"Bitch, you lying! You trying to tell me JP, my fam', sent you at me! I ain't buyin' that lying-ass shit!" B-Low spat and drew back to hit her again.

"It's true, B-Low! JP and a man name Seth want you dead!" Angela screamed, bringing her hands up to cover her bloody face.

When B-Low heard Seth's name, he knew she was telling the truth. His heart dropped; he was truly hurt that his partner, his right-hand man, was the one who'd been betraying him the whole time. "Bitch, get up," B-Low spat as he snatched her up and led her downstairs to the garage.

"B-Low, I'm so, so sorry. Please! I-I love you," she cried as he pushed her along.

"You fuck-ass ho! Who you take me for? Now shut the fuck up!" B-Low screamed, angrier at JP than at Angela.

When he reached the garage, he grabbed some duct tape and bound Angela's wrist and ankles, then laid her naked body on the cool concrete floor. He then rushed back upstairs to get dressed and make a phone call. He heard Angela screaming from all the way upstairs, so on his way out, he planned to tape her mouth shut.

"Yo, Low, what up?" Ranjan answered.

"You with Jack? I need some trash cleaned up out at my crib. I'll leave the garage door unlocked," B-Low said as he plotted his next move.

"A'ight. We on. I got you. I'll hit Jack up, but is it like the last clean-up?" Ranjan asked, referring to the removal of Casey's from the office.

"Pretty much, I'm leavin' you with all the honors on this one too. I'll holla," he said as went back downstairs.

B-Low was disgusted by it all, and he needed to get out and think for a minute.

As soon as he hit the garage door, Angela began begging and pleading for her life, but B-Low turned a dead ear to it all.

"Bitch, fuck you," were his last words to her as he taped her mouth shut. Then he opened the door and stepped out into the cold night air, leaving her for his clean-up crew to deal with.

Chapter 16

It was late, and there'd still been no word from Angela. JP paced the room, waiting for his phone to
ring. She had sounded funny the last time they'd spoken,
kind of nervous or something. JP had a sneaking suspicion that she'd had a change of mind and had just run off
with his money. It was far past the time when she should
have called to let him know the dirty deed had been done.
JP hated to call B-Low at that time of night to see if he'd
heard from Angela, but the suspense was just too much.

"Hello?" B-Low answered, all cool and calm like
everything was all right.

"Boy, what it do? I'm just hittin' you up to make
sure everything was all good with the drop," JP asked,
surprised and angry to hear that B-Low was still alive to
answer his call.

"Yeah, everything all good on that end. I'm 'bout to
head out and grab something to eat. I was trying to see
what our old fuck-buddy Angela's up to. She called a

while ago and said she was gonna fall through, but she ain't never showed up. Bad as I wanted some of that good pussy, that bitch stood me up!" B-Low said, trying his best not to blow his cool.

"Whattt? Angela? Shit, I ain't heard from her in a minute. She stood you up? Boy, you gotta call in your reserves then," JP said, pissed that Angela had backed out and run off with his money after all. *Fuck that lying-ass, thieving bitch! When I catch up to her…*

"For sho. Oh, by the way, we got a meeting tomorrow out at the old warehouse. I done found out who the rat is. You ain't gonna believe it, bro," B-Low spat.

"Who is it?" JP asked curiously, knowing that Grump, Kap, Yella, or Nikki was about to be killed because of him.

"Man, you woulda thought this muthafucker's the one who's been betraying the organization this whole time. But look, bro, I ain't gonna spoil the surprise over the phone. I'm even gonna let you do the honors," B-Low told JP as he navigated his Excursion through the streets of Fulton County, still bitterly surprised by JP's deceit and disloyalty.

"So you finally caught the rat, huh? Shit, I can't wait to make the bitch holla. What time is the meeting?" JP asked, still trying to figure out where Angela had run off to.

"At 5:00. Make sure you tell everybody else to be there, but don't tell them why. I'll get at ya," B-Low told him. As soon as he ended the call with JP, he dialed Ranjan's number to make sure Angela had been taken care of, but he didn't get an answer.

* * *

Back at B-Low's crib, Ranjan and Jack were backing the van up in front of the garage door.

Jack jumped out of the truck and pulled the door open and was surprised to see the trash they'd been called to clean up was a woman.

Angela lay in the middle of the garage floor, all taped up and squirming around like a rodent.

Jack walked up and stood over her, trying his best to keep his excitement under wraps as he looked down at the thick, fine, completely naked dime-piece looking up at him with teary doe eyes, red and swollen. "Damn, lady! Who you piss off?" Jack asked jokingly, taken by Angela's beauty.

"The wrong muthafucker," Ranjan answered, stepping around the van to inspect the trash for himself.

Angela tried to plead with both men, but the tape had her words muffled.

Jack knelt down and pulled the tape from her mouth.

"Please help me! Please! I don't wanna die!" she cried.

Jack and Ranjan looked down at her then at one another.

"Can't spare her, bro, no matter what. We got a job to do, and we sticking to it," Jack said firmly.

Angela cried softly, and Jack could tell her sobbing was bothering Ranjan quite a bit.

"Man, you know I don't do no women or kids. Look

at her, man. She ain't no fuckin' threat. What this li'l bitch gonna do?" Ranjan spat, looking down at the seemingly helpless girl, naked and bloodied and bound on the cold cement.

"Man, you know B-Low don't allow no compromising," Jack said. He reached over and grabbed Angela's neck and was about to snap it and put her out of her misery, but Ranjan grabbed him by the back of his.

"Let the bitch go, man! We ain't killing no broad!" Ranjan screamed, tightening his grip on Jack's neck. Ranjan knew when he grabbed Jack that it was going to be trouble, but he refused to just sit idly by and let his partner kill a helpless, beautiful woman.

Jack became furious. In no time, he reversed the move and broke the hold the inexperienced Ranjan had on him. Ranjan tried to counter, but he was no match for the martial arts expert. Jack broke him down with ease, and seconds later, he had Ranjan in a death grip, slowly cutting off his air. Furious at Ranjan's actions, he applied more and more pressure to his windpipe, until he couldn't breathe at all.

Angela was stunned as she watched the man kill his partner, her would-be hero, and she knew for a fact that she would be next. She silently rooted for Ranjan, but it was no use.

Jack was a real killer, and Ranjan had been developing a conscience as of late—something that didn't exactly go hand in hand in their line of work. Jack knew his one-time partner had become a weak link, so he continued to apply more pressure, until the man was dead. He then released his grip on Ranjan's neck and walked back over to finish the job.

"Please no! Ahhh! Please!" Angela screamed at the top of her lungs, but seconds later, those same two murderous large hands wrapped around her neck and started squeezing. She couldn't breathe. Everything went black as she wiggled around like a fish out of water, trying to get away from the hands that showed no mercy. Her bowels moved as her life was seized.

Jack wiped the sweat from his forehead as he surveyed the damage. He quickly loaded both bodies into the van and headed out to the dumping spot, deciding that he'd explain it all to B-Low later.

* * *

An hour after riding around, gathering his thoughts and putting his plans together, B-Low pulled up at his house. Before going inside, he looked in the garage to make sure the trash had been properly disposed of. When he saw that his garage floor was vacant of bodies, he made a mental note to make a deposit the next morning to pay for a job well done.

Chapter 17

The next morning, JP was in the car early, heading over to Angela's place to see if she was there. He had left her numerous messages and sent several texts, but she hadn't responded to any of them. He slapped the steering wheel, mad at himself for agreeing to pay her half up front. When he pulled up to her spot, he noticed her car wasn't there, so he didn't bother to get out. Not knowing what else to think or do, he decided to put in a call to B-Low to see if he was alive.

"Hello?" B-Low answered groggily, looking over at the time on his bedside clock.

JP cursed under his breath when B-Low answered. "Oh, uh, hey, bro. I just wanted to confirm the meeting at 5:00," JP stuttered, furious that B-Low was still living and finally convinced that Angela had indeed scammed him out of the money for a job she didn't do.

"Yeah, 5:00, bro. I'll holla," B-Low replied before he rolled over and drifted back to sleep.

"Fuck!" JP screamed. He slammed his cell phone down in the passenger seat, furious with himself for making the decision to bring Angela into his plans. He was now behind, and there was no way he was going to meet the deadline of getting rid of B-Low before the weekend. He looked at his watch and saw that it was past 9:00, so he put in a call to Seth.

"Yo, friend. How's life?" Seth asked in a sarcastic tone.

"I need more time," JP uttered as he pushed the Lexus past the speed limit, heading back home.

"No. I've given you more than enough time to take care of this shit. You're nothing but a bumbling idiot nigger! You and the whole organization will be dealt with for this!" Seth snapped, then hung up the phone.

JP had never been one to take a threat lightly. He exited off the ramp and turned around to head to Seth's car lot. He loaded his .45 automatic as he weaved in and out of traffic. JP was past his breaking point, and Angela's betrayal and Seth's cruel threat had taken him there. He was going to do something he'd been wanting to do for the longest time. *How dare Seth make a threat on me? I'm gonna kill that muthafucker.*

Twenty minutes later, JP was pulling up into the car lot. The place was devoid of customers, and the only two cars there besides the one for sale were Seth's and Jody's. After bringing the Lexus to a screeching halt, JP jumped out and headed for the office in a hurry. Jody and Seth was going over paperwork when he pushed the door open with the .45 in his grip.

"Whoa! Hold up now, buddy!" Seth called out as JP

burst through the door.

Pop! Pop! Pop! the .45 spat, catching Jody once in the face and lodging two bullets in his torso until he coughed up blood and fell to the floor.

"Wait a minute! Hold up, friend!" Seth called out, shocked at the sight of his right-hand man lying there in a widening puddle of blood.

JP walked over and stood over a cowering Seth. "Naw, nigga. You said I'm a dead man, right?" JP said, putting the gun to Seth's head.

"Hold on, JP. Let's be sensible about this situation. If you walk out of here now, I'll give you not one, but *two* territories. Matter of fact, take these. It's all yours, buddy," Seth called out, handing him the keys to the brand new Phantom.

"I'm good. Fuck nigga, " JP said forcefully as he pulled the trigger on the .45. He watched as the hollow-point made a small hole in Seth's head, blowing out a chunk of the man's skull when it made its exit; Seth fell head first onto his custom-made desk with a *thud*.

JP turned and walked out to find Angela, next on his list.

The federal agent sitting outside called in a uniformed officer to check out the car lot office after he heard the shots. He'd been warned by his superiors that he couldn't risk blowing his cover under any circumstances, so he stayed in place and followed a good length behind JP, one of the many main players unknowingly involved in Operation Down Low.

eanwhile, Real was busy taking the city by storm. He'd gotten back in touch with many of his old clientele, and he'd gladly discovered that the majority of them had also changed their game to heroin. The money began rolling just like old times, and Real began feeling himself again.

As he pushed the Dodge Ram through the heart of the city, he thought about Cash, his right-hand man. Cash had been like a brother to him, but then he'd turned snitch. He picked up his phone and dialed his old friend Frog.

"Speak ya mind," Frog called out, his usual way of answering the phone.

"Yo, Frog, what it is?" Real barked into the phone.

"Not the Real deal! Man, where you been, playa?" Frog replied, happy to hear from his old associate.

"Bro, I had to pull a bid. I ain't been back home long. I'm trying to get in touch with that boy Cash. You seen him around lately?" Real asked, almost tasting the revenge.

"Man, Cash got killed not long after you disappeared from the scene. A nigga down in Macon hit him up while he was sitting at a red light. You believe dat shit? A stripper bitch he was fucking with was killed up the street in a hotel room they'd rented for the weekend. They say it was the bitch baby-daddy who did it. Anyway, yeah, that nigga Cash been dead for a minute," Frog said.

Real was surprised by the news, but he wasn't exactly saddened by it. "Damn. What about that boy B-Low, that one who used to run with Jesse?" Real asked curiously.

"I remember B-Low and Jesse, them robbing-ass li'l niggas. B-Low ain't to be fucked with now though. That boy done got his weight up, and he ain't bullshitting. Some nigga tried to take 'im out the game a while ago, so now he walking around with two bodyguards. He done killed a whole lotta niggas, man," Frog complained.

"Where he making his thang jump at?" Real asked, glad B-Low would finally get his due.

"He out on the south side mostly, but the nigga is coast to coast too. I fuck with his lieutenant nigga a little. They call him JP. I can holla at him and get him to get B-Low to get at ya if ya want," Frog said, hoping his cooperation would somehow earn him some brownie points with the man who'd once run the city and might be back to doing it again.

"Naw, that's a'ight. I'll catch up with him later. I'll holla if I need your help. Meantime, be easy, bro," Real said, ending the call with enough info to go after B-Low.

Real rode through a couple of his old spots, checking the scene. Things hadn't changed much while he'd been away. He dipped out of the 'hood and rode out to the nicer parts of the city, in search of a new residence. He planned to keep the rat hole he already had; he could use it as his dope spot. After riding around a while, he found a nice set of condos off Highway 138. He wrote down the address and phone number from the sign out front.

After that, Real headed back to his temporary home to check his daily take and his inventory. On the way, he made a pit stop at the corner store up the street from the 'hood where he lived. "Y'all got any big Ziploc bags? I only see the small ones over there," Real asked the Chinese man behind the counter.

"We no have big. Only what you see. No bigs," he replied, looking at Real suspiciously

Real shrugged off the man's odd, paranoid expression and exited.

As soon as he stepped out the door, a man approached him, trying to make a buck. "Yo, bro, man, check this out! I got somethin' for you on the low-low. You can't beat dat wit' a stick!" the man said, showing Real the gold watch on his wrist.

The watch was some knock-off cheap shit that didn't even begin to catch Real's attention. The tattoo on the man's hand, however, did catch his eye. *Jazz? Shit. Yeah, muthafucker, I've seen you before.* Real smiled and took the man up on his offer. "Yeah, that's a nice watch. I'll take it, but I ain't got no cash on me, man. Can you follow me out to my spot?" Real asked sincerely.

The fool took the watch off his wrist. "Man, I'm on my bike, but I—"

"That's all right. I'm just right around the corner. Hop in. I'll give you a ride back when we're done," Real said, cutting the man off and vividly remembering being robbed and hit in the head with a pistol.

"A'ight," the man agreed, without saying another word.

Real walked back over to the truck and unlocked the passenger door for the man to get in. "How much you want for it?" Real asked as he climbed behind the steering wheel and pulled the truck in drive.

"For you, fam', $250…and that's way below what this mug worth," the man said, pitching like a true salesman full of bullshit.

"Okay. Yeah, that's a good deal," Real agreed. He smiled at the man, then carefully reached down in his side door panel and grabbed the .357 he always kept tucked in there just in case.

The man eyed Real suspiciously and started to say something, but he couldn't get a word out before the gun was shoved in his face. "Man, come on! Man, if this is about this shitty watch, you can have it! It's yours! Please!" he screamed and started to shake.

Real pulled the truck up in the alley just around the corner from a local drug spot, an alley known as The Graveyard due to the countless murder victims and un-identifiable bodies that turned up there.

The man looked around and recognized where they were, much to his dismay. "Yo, bro, spare me! What's up with this shit, my nigga?" he asked as the truck came to a stop in the back of the alley. "I swear I didn't hurt the broad. I just took the watch and—"

"Don't you remember me? Nigga, you just robbed me the other day in front of Club Candlewood. You hit me in the damn head with yo' sorry-ass li'l pistol! Well, now it's my time, you—"

"Wait! Hold up, man. If I did that, I'm sorry, man. C'mon, my nigga. You know how the game go. A man's gotta try to eat," he pleaded as he looked down the barrel of the .357 Magnum.

"Yeah, I do know how the game go, so this is what I'm gonna do. You're gonna open the door, and I'm gonna give you a ten-second head start before I come after you. If I catch you, I'm gonna kill you. If you somehow manage to get away, we'll just write the shit off. Is that fair enough for you?" Real asked and smiled.

"Uh…yeah," the man stuttered as he positioned himself to take off.

"Don't go until I say so, you understand?" Real asked firmly.

"Okay, man. Just let me know when," the man replied nervously, positioning himself in the open door of the truck.

"Okay. On three. One…two…three!" Real screamed.

But just as the man squared up and turned to jump out, a loud *Boom*! rang out.

The .357 bullet tore through the back of the man's head and came out the front, tearing his whole face off in the process. The force of the shot sent him face first out of the truck, right onto the concrete.

Real reached over, closed the door, and drove off to head home. "Bitch-ass nigga," he whispered under his breath as he turned on his street.

Chapter 19

*M*ichael was the talk of the cartel. The way he'd mishandled the hit on Real was unacceptable in many of their eyes, but he couldn't be outright punished for it because he was the head of one of the strongest family in the circle.

Angelo and Milo sat in Mizelo's, an old Italian eatery that was frequented by members of the cartel. They discussed Michael and the disrespectful way he'd handled the retribution for their uncles' demise.

"Look, Angelo, this muthafucker has disrespected our families, and the only thing he's got to say about it is… well, nothing. He hasn't even offered to give our money back for the botched-up job. I'm gonna make that fucker pay with his life!" Milo screamed, causing the other patrons in the restaurant to turn their heads away from their pasta and look in their direction.

"Shh! God, hold it down. Shit's got to be handled discreetly. All that acting without thinking ain't gonna work. It's only going to get you killed," Angelo said firmly. He'd thought of a way to kill two birds with one stone.

Angelo had never liked Milo, and he hated that he'd been appointed head of the family after their uncles' untimely death. The cartel had welcomed Angelo with open arms, but Milo hadn't been so lucky. A few of the family heads had voiced their less-than-favorable opinion of Milo, but everyone knew he was really the only remaining male capable of running his family, so the other heads had no choice but to vote him in.

Milo knew he was hated by almost everyone at the table, but he didn't care. He absolutely refused to change his renegade ways for the group of "old-fashioned dick-heads," as he liked to call them. "I'm gonna contact Rio on this job. He'll be happy to do it. He's been bugging me for work lately," Milo said as he finished off the rest of his lasagna.

"Look, Milo, it's gotta be done quietly. Better yet, maybe we should just put it before the cartel and see how they feel about it," Angelo cleverly suggested, knowing the other members wouldn't agree with killing Michael, the well-liked head of family.

"The families will never agree, and I'm not waiting for their permission. I'm going to do this for our uncles, and then I'll handle Real myself," Milo snapped as he took a sip of the sweet tea that sat before him.

"Things got to be—."

"Angelo, I ain't got time for your cowardly ass right now . This is about paying respects to our uncles. Maybe you oughtta seek out a new profession. They're hiring a dishwasher here. Can you scrub gravy off pans? 'Cause you sure as hell are too fuckin' soft to be head of a family!" Milo barked.

Angelo looked at him with pure hatred. "Look, you stupid, loud-mouthed prick, I'm much bigger of a man than you'll ever be, a far greater asset to my family than you'll ever be to yours. The next time you disrespect me, you'll be swimming with the fishes. You got that?" Angelo said through clenched teeth.

"Whatever. Just know that Michael *will* pay with his life for this, with or without the consent of the family," Milo replied and then smiled a sinister smile.

"Just make sure that it's clean, with no ties to us," Angelo told Milo as he stood to leave.

"Let me handle this," Milo said, pulling his cell phone from his pocket.

Minutes later, Rio was en route to find Michael at the address Milo had eagerly given him.

After Angelo exited, Milo ordered a stiff drink and just relaxed, waiting for the phone call to confirm that it had been handled, whether the cartel liked it or not.

* * *

Rio leaned to the side in the old Chevy pick-up as he neared the address Milo had given him. Rio had met Michael on a couple of other occasions when Milo had summoned him for a job, so he knew him on sight. He looked for the Italian deli on the corner and spotted it rather quickly.

Inside the deli, Michael was sitting in the back room, going over his books. He handled most of his business in the back of the family deli, in an expensively furnished office.

When Rio pulled up, he looked through the large front window and saw only a young Italian teenager, cutting up sandwich meat and lettuce in preparation for the day's customers. Rio killed the engine on the old pick-up and exited the truck while tucking his Sig Sauer P556 pistol in his jacket. He stepped into the deli and carefully checked out the scene again, then asked the boy behind the counter if Michael was there.

"Uh, yeah, he's in the back, sir, but I think he's real busy," said the chubby boy before he went back to cutting prosciutto into sandwich-thin slices.

Rio walked his six-six, 280-pound frame by the counter and headed to the back, ignoring the boy.

"Sir!" the boy called out, stepped around the counter with a sharp butcher knife in his hand.

Rio stopped and looked at the boy, then proceeded.

The boy foolishly ran up on him, trying to stop him from interrupting Michael.

Having no other choice and knowing the boy could now ID him, Rio pulled the Sig Sauer from his jacket and pointed it at the kid.

The boy eyes grew as big as golf balls, and his voice cracked as he started to speak. "Sir, I just—"

But Rio didn't want to hear it.

Tic! Tic! Tic! Tic! The Sig Sauer spat like an Uzi, its

bullets tearing through the young boy's chest until he looked like the freshly ground Italian sausage on the counter behind him.

As soon as the boy's mutilated body hit the floor, Rio rushed to the back, looking for Michael.

Michael had heard the gunfire in the front of the deli and instinctively reached into his desk drawer for his .38 revolver. He got up, gripping his .38 tightly, and started heading to the front to see what was going on. "Delano!" he screamed, trying to get his dead nephew's attention.

Just as he stepped through the doorway, Rio was stepping in. They shared uneasy eye contact for only a quick second before they both raised their guns. Michael was seconds too slow on the draw. Rio laid the Sig Sauer right up against Michael's face and pulled the trigger. The string of merciless bullets had Michael resembling a bobble-head doll, throwing his skull back and forth as they took turns piercing his brain. Rio didn't stick around to see him drop, but he did hear him hit the floor with a *thump* as he exited the back room. He knew there might be some consequences to pay for his actions, but he didn't realize just how bad they would be.

Chapter 20

After ordering his bodyguards to get rid of Angela's car and other belongings, B-Low headed out to the meeting. He arrived at the warehouse thirty minutes before everyone else, just to make sure everything was set. He had brought a bag of supplies especially for the occasion. Once he was satisfied that all was in order, he took a seat at the old wooden table to wait for the crew to arrive.

The members started arriving one by one, and twenty minutes later, everyone was present and accounted for.

"Everyone please take a seat, and don't worry. We won't be long," B-Low bellowed, his voice echoing through the empty warehouse.

All the members sat down, wondering why the emergency meeting had been called. JP sat next to B-Low.

B-Low pushed out his chair and stood to address his crew. "Everybody listen and listen good! As you all know, we've got a rat in the house, and we've been after this rat for some time. Well, I've finally figured out who he is, and it turns out the rat is somebody sitting in this room!" B-Low screamed as he pulled out his plastic sixteen-shot Glock.

Kap, Yella, Nikki, Grump, and JP looked around at each other suspiciously as B-Low walked around the table, staring at each and every one of them, like some sick-ass game of Duck-Duck-Goose.

"You know, when we all joined this organization, we promised loyalty and dedication to each other and the cause!" B-Low screamed as he slammed his fist on the table in between Kap and Nikki, causing them to jump.

"Rat, you know who you are, and you will be handled accordingly!" JP added, looking menacingly at each other member of the crew.

"You're right about that, JP. I'm gonna make the rat wish he'd never crossed me," B-Low spoke calmly this time as he made his way around the table, each member still watching him intently.

Everyone at the table thought about Casey, the man who'd been assassinated for his betrayal.

B-Low walked back around the table again. This time, he stopped directly behind JP and raised his pistol, causing everyone's eyes to widen with surprise.

JP didn't pick up on it until he felt the cold barrel of the weapon against the back of his head. "Wh-wh-what the hell's going on, bro?" JP yelled as he started to get up.

"Nigga, sit down. You move again, and I'm gonna blow your fuckin' head off!" B-Low spat, patting him down like a cop and pulling his pistol from his waistband.

"Man, what the hell are you doing, bro! Low, you know I'd never betray you. You my nigga, I swear! C'mon now. Don't even do it like this, man," JP pleaded, still trying his best to convince B-Low that he was mistaken.

"Nigga, shut the fuck up! You remember that bitch Angela? She's been taken out with the trash. How you gonna have the nerve to send a bitch after me?" B-Low spat as he slammed the butt of the gun on the top of JP's head, causing him to fall out of the chair.

"Damn, B, this nigga was the one?" Kap asked, rising from his own chair and pulling his gun.

"Fo' real, bitch-ass nigga?" Grump added, also standing.

Yella and Nikki couldn't believe JP, the man they'd looked up to for so long, had betrayed them all. They both stood and walked over to JP, who was still dazed from the blow to the head.

"Look, man, I don't know what Angela told you, bro, but I ain't have nothing to do with no—"

Smack!

The blow to JP's jaw instantly brought blood. He spat out red, salty saliva, along with chips of his broken tooth.

"Y'all get this rat and tie him up real good in a chair," B-Low ordered, tossing Yella a roll of duct tape from his goodie bag.

"Low, come on, man! I swear it weren't me, dog! It's Yella, dog! Him and that ho Angela's hooked up more than once. They gotta be the ones, dog! Please hold up, man!" JP screamed.

Yella took a cheap shot as Grump, Kap, and Nikki dragged JP over to the chair and started taping him in.

B-Low pulled a pair of pliers and a blowtorch from the bag while JP was being secured to the chair.

"Nigga, I trusted you! You…you…you fuckin' lying-ass nigga!" B-Low screamed as he hit JP in the face with the blowtorch.

"Ow! Low, man, it ain't me, man!" JP cried, spitting more blood from his busted mouth.

B-Low pulled the striker from the bag and lit the blowtorch. He then positioned the flame just inches away from JP'S nose. "Nigga, you done fucked up," B-Low told him as he touched the tip of JP's nose with the red, yellow, and blue flame.

"Ahhhhhh! Ah, man!" JP screamed out in pain, his nose cooking like a piece of meat.

The crew looked on and turned their nose up at the stench of the burning flesh.

B-Low took his time burning JP's nose, fingers, ears, and lips. After administering pain with the blowtorch for half an hour, he tossed the pliers to Yella and told him to pull his teeth. "Nigga, they ain't never gonna be able to identify your punk ass!" B-Low spat as he watched Yella take the pliers to JP's front teeth.

"Ahhhhhh! Oh ple…God, please!" JP stuttered and screamed as his teeth were ruthlessly jerked out one by one.

"I'm sick of looking at this fucker. Put the plastic bag on his head," B-Low instructed Nikki.

Nikki pulled the plastic bag over his head and taped it at the bottom, dodging the steady stream of blood running down his face.

The blood and the stench of the burning flesh had the warehouse smelling like death. JP struggled to breathe inside the bag, blowing it in and out. The shock was setting in, and he was getting weak.

The crew stood back and watched him struggling to breathe, the man they'd all admired just earlier that very same day.

"Let's go," B-Low told the crew as he grabbed the gas can and poured gas all over JP, once his right-hand man.

JP shook his head side to side, trying to beg B-Low not to do it, but B-Low only smiled.

Just as the crew turned to walk away, B-Low tossed a match on JP's lap. It quickly ignited the fuel, engulfing his helpless body in flames. The plastic bag melted to his flesh before the flames flicked up and consumed his skin, muscles, eyes, cartilage, and bones. His screams could be heard faintly from outside the abandoned warehouse as the crew got in their vehicles and headed out.

But B-Low and his crew were not the only ones who saw the smoke signals coming from the building. The federal agents quickly radioed for assistance as they followed B-Low and his vengeful crew out of the lot.

Chapter 21

The next day, all the cartel families were called together for an emergency meeting because of two murders: the head of a family and his poor, young nephew, who wasn't guilty of anything besides occasionally slicing a tomato too thick. As the men filled the home of Carasco, suspicion was passed around about the person responsible. The Bonatello family had threatened Michael just a week prior, frustrated by Michael's control of a territory they once had a stronghold in. Every family had representatives in attendance, and they planned to pool their resources to find whoever was responsible and make them pay.

Angelo looked across the table at Milo, who didn't show any sign of guilt as he took his seat.

"Everybody, as we know, a beloved family member was murdered in cold blood in his place of business. His little nephew Delano was also killed during this vile, unauthorized attack. It's no secret that the Bonatello family had made subtle threats on Michael's life, but that threat has now been carried out. Today, I need each of you to put your handymen on standby. We will—and I repeat, we *will*—strike back and strike back hard to let them know we are still the strongest families in this region. We can't take these people lightly, men. They just cut down one of our own without hesitation. Clearly, they are ready for a war."

Milo and Angelo made brief eye contact again as Carasco vented about Michael's death and continued blaming the Bonatellos.

What if they knew it was Milo who did it? Angelo fantasized to himself.

Milo cast Angelo a serious you-talk-you-die look, and Angelo picked up on it quickly and smiled back at him as if to brag that he had him by the balls.

All the men in the room gave Carasco their undivided attention as he went over his plan of attack.

"Our handymen will be there to take his sorry ass out while he's having dinner at his favorite spot, Geneve. Make sure you tell your men not to spare anyone this time, women and children included if they get in the way," Carasco told the room as he pulled off his glasses and pushed them down into his jacket pocket.

Everyone was in agreement with the plan of action Carasco had put together.

Angelo knew it was not the right time to expose Milo and his dirty deed, so he kept quiet and went along with Carasco.

"By tomorrow evening, Bonatello and his people will be lying in pools of their own greedy blood!" Carasco said, calling for the adjournment of the meeting so everyone could make the contacts they needed to make and give the go-ahead to take out all members of the Bonatello family.

As everybody mixed and mingled, Angelo fell back and ducked off into the restroom. Pulling out his phone, he dialed Carasco's cell number.

"Yes? May I help you?" Carasco asked as he stood around and mingled with the remaining family members.

"You've got the wrong man. Milo killed Michael," Angelo said, disguising his voice. Then he hastily hung up the phone and eased out of the bathroom, right back into the crowd.

Carasco flipped his phone closed and looked at it in confusion. "Gentlemen!" Carasco called out, thinking about what the mysterious caller had told him.

The whole room fell silent as Carasco deep voice boomed off the high ceilings and walls.

Carasco looked for Milo in the crowd, making sure the possible traitor was still in attendance. "Could you all just give me a few more minutes of your time? Fredo, please accompany us," Carasco called out. He waited for his personal security guard, a six-one, 250-pound killer, to enter the room before he started.

All the men looked confused as Fredo entered the room; civilians (anyone who wasn't a family head) were never allowed in their meetings, and on top of that, none of them knew what the second random meeting could possibly be about. Carasco didn't know who the caller was, but they had to have inside information, because they had called his carefully restricted personal number. After he thought about what the caller had said, it began to make sense to him. He knew the Bonatello family would never be so reckless in their actions, especially after openly making threats. On top of that, if they had done it, they would have sent a message after the fact to make a point, but that hadn't been done. The more he thought about it, the more he felt Milo could have been responsible. He hoped he wasn't mistaken in making such a severe accusation, for that would be very detrimental to his own position. "Men, I'm sorry for the inconvenience, but I've just received some very important information from an inside source," Carasco announced, looking around the room and pausing his gaze on Milo.

Angelo looked over at Fredo and knew exactly what was about to go down. All the men in the room professed to be equal in power, but everyone knew the made man Carasco was the most powerful man in the room. All of them looked up to him and admired him.

Milo looked up and realized Carasco was staring right at him. Then he disregarded the ludicrous thought, thinking he was just being paranoid. He knew he had gone against all the family rules by having Michael put down, but he also knew there was no way the families could tie him to the killing.

"Men, I've just been informed…" Carasco started, but then he stopped and called Fredo over and whispered something in his ear.

Fredo looked up and frowned, then set his sights directly on Milo.

Milo noticed the extra attention he was getting, and he started putting it all together: the special meeting, Fredo's presence, all the whispering, and all the glares and stares directed at him. He started to sweat and fidget, knowing the meeting was about him. He knew if he sat there any longer, he'd be called out, questioned, and most likely killed for the murder of a made man. Milo checked the scene and squirmed, anxious to see his way out. Fredo wasn't by the exit any longer, so Milo took this time to make his break.

Angelo noticed the nervousness in Milo. He half-smiled, glad that the incompetent Milo was about to be taken care of.

"Excuse me, men, but as I was saying, I have just discovered that…" Carasco started again as Fredo started in Milo's direction.

Milo didn't hesitate any longer.

"…the man responsible for…"

Crash!

Milo jumped up out of his chair, causing it to crash to the floor, then scrambled to the exit door.

"Stop him!" Carasco called out to the room as Milo ran by them and out the door.

Fredo was hot on his heels as the other men in the room looked on in total disbelief, realizing that Milo was, in fact, responsible for murdering one of their own.

"Men, Milo is entirely to blame for Michael's and his nephew's deaths!" Carasco yelled. He and all the other men rushed out the room in hot pursuit of Milo, who was quickly making his way across the back yard, trying to head for the woods.

Fredo was right behind him, stride for stride, closing

in.

Milo knew the bigger, younger man wasn't going to give up, for Fredo was athletic and long-winded. When he reached the manmade lake, he stopped, helplessly watching Fredo running in his direction. Milo pulled his revolver from his inside jacket pocket and hid behind a big oak tree, waiting for Fredo to get closer.

Fredo knew Milo couldn't have gone far with the lake in the way, so he slowed to a light jog and took a look around. He knew Milo had to be close. He patted his jacket and was none too pleased to realize that he must have dropped his gun. As soon as he turned to pass the big oak tree, Milo jumped out and fired. The bullet hit Fredo in the side of the head, sending him sideways as his head exploded. His big body crumpled to the ground in a heap.

As soon as Milo saw the other men coming his way, he took off again. He slid through the neighbor's yard and disappeared.

The made men stopped when they reached Fredo's body. They pulled their cell phones out and started making calls, telling their men that they wanted Milo dead on sight.

Milo exited the woods and walked briskly down the long, winding road that stretched for miles and miles out. Every time he saw a car headed in his direction, he ducked back into the woods until it passed. As he walked, he wondered how in the hell the families knew he was responsible for Michael's murder. He planned to get to the bottom of it later, but for the time being, he had to get as far away from Florida as he could.

As he walked, he saw a car coming in his direction.

It didn't take him long to recognize Angelo's bright red Ferrari F430 Spider speeding in his direction. Milo breathed a sigh of relief when he saw that Angelo was alone. He darted out of the woods to the middle of the street, waving his arms frantically, trying to get Angelo's attention.

Angelo noticed someone in the middle of the street ahead of him. To be on the safe side, he pulled his chrome Desert Eagle from the console and put it in his lap. The closer he got, the easier it was to recognize the panicking pedestrian in front of him. When he got within a few yards, he saw that the man was Milo. Angelo pulled to the side of the road.

"Man, I'm glad to see you. I don't know how they found out I—" Milo stopped midsentence as Angelo pointed the Desert Eagle at him from the driver seat. "Angelo, what the hell are you doing?" Milo asked, positioning himself to take off into the woods. But Angelo didn't give him the chance to run. "Milo, I'm gonna do something I shoulda done a long time ago," he said just before he pulled the trigger.

Milo was unprepared as the bullets did their job and pierced his chest and heart. He said something inaudible and the fell backward.

Angelo smiled, pulled out his cell phone, and made the call to Carasco to give him the good news. "Twin Orchard Road. Milo is all yours," he said, taking one last look out his window at the body. *All in a day's work,* he thought before he raced the red Ferrari up the street, en route to his golf outing.

G STREET CHRONICLES
A NEW URBAN DYNASTY

WWW.GSTREETCHRONICLES.COM

Chapter 22

$\mathcal{R}$eal thought about what Frog had told him about B-Low, walking around with bodyguards. It didn't matter to Real if the Secret Service had the asshole's back; he was still going to make him pay. Frog had also filled him in on B-Low's favorite hangouts, like Justin's in downtown Atlanta and Sexy in the City, the new Buckhead strip club B-Low had invested in. Real planned to hit both spots as soon as the sun went down, determined to see B-Low face to face before he killed him. He wanted to look at the man responsible for his baby's death and let him know why he had to die. Real couldn't get Constance's cries out of his head, and the more he replayed them over and over, the madder he got.

Strapping up in all black, Real exited his spot and jumped behind the wheel of the truck. His first stop was going to be Justin's; Puff himself was supposed to be in the house that night, but that wasn't the VIP Real was looking for.

As he drove down 285, Real toyed with the .357 Cobra, thinking back on how his life had changed. Now that his money was back to good, he planned to handle his unfinished business, then kick back and rebuild his life.

Thirty minutes later, he was pulling up in Justin's parking lot. The place was packed. He scanned the lot, looking for the Lexus Frog had told him B-Low usually drove. When he didn't see Low's vehicle, he got out and took a quick look inside the restaurant. He got a couple of stares from the customers as he strolled through the establishment, dressed in all black. Once he was sure B-Low wasn't at Justin's, he headed back to the truck to go to Sex in the City.

Pulling up in the Sex in the City parking lot was like pulling into a car show. The lot was filled with all makes and models of expensive customized vehicles. Real took two spins around the lot before he found a parking space next to a tinted-out black Yukon. As he made his way to the front entrance of the club, he noticed the big Lexus with "Low 357" plates; it was parked right in the front. Real knew then that B-Low was in the club.

"Agent Hurley, do you have a visual?" He scanned the parking lot from the black-tinted Yukon.

"Ten-four. Suspect is headed to the back office. Looks like he's got an unknown female with him," replied the undercover agent who was positioned inside the club.

The club was filled with undercover agents—eleven, to be exact—in position to take down the man believed to be highly responsible for the city's embarrassing increased crime rate. They all zeroed in on his back office and awaited the next set of instructions.

"We're securing the lot now. As soon as we finish, we'll radio you to initiate the take-down."

"Ten-four."

Real stood in line to enter the club, hating that he'd had to leave his heat behind. He couldn't wait to get face to face with B-Low, and he planned to trick him into coming outside so he could blow his brains all over the parking lot.

As Real entered the club, the FBI agents got in position to rush the back office, where B-Low was now entertaining Sundae, the half-black, half-white freak, an ex porn star.

"Everybody confirm your positions. We're moving in on three!" said the agent in his Yukon, speaking into his walkie-talkie. On the count of three, he and his partner exited the truck and walked briskly up to the front door.

Walking through the club, Real thought twice about trying to trick B-Low into going outside. He was sure B-Low was smarter than that; he'd never go for it, and even if he did, his security goons would be right by his side. Real knew he had to think of a better way to get at B-Low. By the time he got to the rear of the club, where the office most likely was, he'd thought of a better idea. Just as Real was about to make his move to the office, he heard someone yelling. Seconds later, a line of official men came rushing back in his direction. Real was very familiar with the orders they were barking, so he moved to the side to let them by. They rushed passed him on their way back to B-Low's office. Real found a safe corner and watched. Seconds later, the men came out with B-Low in handcuffs. As they escorted him through the club, all the patrons looked on.

Just as the head-hanging B-Low walked by, Real called his name, and he lifted his head. It was as if he saw a ghost. Real stood there, proud and tall, looking at him with utter disgust on his face. B-Low shook his head and did a double take. He couldn't believe Real was in his club, and he silently thanked the police because he knew they'd saved him from the man dressed in black.

Real walked out behind the group of police and federal agents and watched as they loaded B-Low into the waiting police cruiser. He was beyond pissed, knowing his revenge would have to be delayed, but he would still get it, one way or another. Real had made his beloved Constance a promise, and he planned to stick to it.

Chapter 23

*A*ngelo sat at his bedroom computer desk and pulled up a map of Atlanta. After taking notes on all the spots Real was supposed to have lived, he picked up the phone and called Blanco. "Hey, my friend. Long time, no hear. I got a job for you in Atlanta. It needs to be taken care of quickly," Angelo told his longtime assassin, a man who openly lived for his next kill like junkies live for their next high. "You up for it?"

"Always. Info?" Blanco asked, hoping the job wouldn't require a lot of grunt work. He liked to get to his victims and dispose of them quickly, without a lot of red tape.

Angelo knew Blanco was very familiar with the man in question because he'd been commissioned to kill the man's girlfriend a year earlier. Real had been stuck in prison while Blanco had sat back in the upscale, quiet neighborhood, watching B-Low's house, the place where Constance had been staying. It had turned out to be just his luck that she exited the house in a hurry on her cell phone and walked right into his web. Blanco hadn't been back to Atlanta since the night of the killing, but he had no qualms of paying the city a visit again.

Angelo gave Blanco all the information he had on Real and reminded him that it was imperative that he handle the job ASAP. Angelo had a lot on his plate, but at least he'd gotten rid of one little problem.

The made men had shown up five minutes after Angelo had departed the scene, only to find Milo in a puddle of his own blood. They made preparations to have him dumped into the Everglades. Carasco and the other men commended Angelo on taking Milo out, but Angelo knew his job was only halfway done. Now he wanted Real, and wasn't going to stop until the man was shot and killed in the streets like a rabid dog. He knew Blanco would find Real and take him out with ease, so he just sat back and waited after the call had been made.

Chapter 24

"   *I* don't know what y'all trying to do, but you must be totally mistaken," B-Low told the officers as they pulled up outside of the Rice Street jail.

"Yeah, yeah. That's what they all say," the young, black, gung-ho officer said as he parked the squad car and got out. "He's got an outstanding warrant, so I'm going to book him on it as well as all the other state charges we've got. Then you feds can have whatever's left of the muthafucker," the officer told the two federal agents who'd followed him to the station.

"Okay. I'll inform my superiors that we have him in custody. I just hate that we couldn't make his partner, this, uh…JP, pay before he killed him. We've got plenty of other agents out rounding up the rest of the scum-bag crew," the tall, slender, older, white veteran agent told the officer, glancing over at B-Low, who sat in the back of the squad car with his head down. "That boy ain't ever gonna see daylight again."

"You're right about that. What we've got on his ass will send him away until he's good and old, and then y'all can bust him with federal charges and pick out his casket after his trial. He's never gonna set foot outside prison walls again," the officer said proudly as he walked over and opened the squad car door to get B-Low out.

"C'mon, you sorry-ass fucker. We got you."

"Man, y'all got the wrong man. I need to call my lawyer," B-Low spat as he was led into the jail and placed in a holding cell.

"Man, fuck a lawyer! You're gonna need God, Allah, and Buddha to save yo' ass. Shit. You out there running around taking your own kind down while you riding around in yo' fancy car with yo' fancy clothes while muthafuckas killing and robbing to get that shit you selling. That's why all these kids are fucked up now, because of your sorry, greedy, inhuman ass. But don't worry 'bout that no mo'. B-Low my ass. You gon' be *below* ground by the time you done serving your jail time. It's over for you, son."

The young officer slammed the cell door, had another laugh at B-Low's expense, and went back over to the booking desk to process the paperwork on the file that was at least an inch thick.

"Fuck!" B-Low screamed out loud as the door closed and the reality of it all set in.

"What the fuck! Kill that loud shit, my nigga. Don't you know a nigga gotta sleep up in here?" snapped a young wannabe rapper. He'd been brought in for aggravated assault, and he was trying to get comfortable on the hard steel bench.

"Nigga, who the fuck you talking to? Bitch-ass nigga!"

B-Low screamed angrily, anxious to release his frustration on somebody.

"What! Bitch-ass nigga? I'm gonna show you a bitch, nigga!" the young six-one, 215-pound thug called out, rising up off the bench.

B-Low didn't hesitate. He pounced on the young thug before he could get two feet on the ground.

Clunk! Smack!

It was on as B-Low rained blows to the thug's head and face. After the first flurry of blows, B-Low was surprised to see that the young boy was still in the mix. B-Low went hard, but the thug wouldn't lie down.

Out of nowhere, the thug threw a haymaker, catching B-Low just right, dazing him and causing him to stumble back. That gave the thug the chance he needed to come at Low swiftly, as if he'd been fighting for a living. He hit B-Low with a two-piece, knocking him to the ground, then kicked him in the face.

B-Low tried his best to recover, but the kid was coming too hard and fast. B-Low knew he was in a no-win situation, so he did the only thing he could.

"Heeelp! Guard!" B-Low yelled as he curled into a ball trying to protect himself from the hard licks coming his way.

The jailers heard someone screaming from Holding Cell 2. It was normal for fights to break out, but they could tell this scream was a real plea for help, so they decided to check it out. As soon as they got to the cell, they could see how serious it was. Blood was everywhere, and the man they'd just booked into the jail was out cold.

"Get down NOW!" the jailers screamed as they cuffed the young thug and radioed for medical assistance.

Chapter 25

"She loves me, she loves me not," Blanco sang out while playing with his different hunting knives while on his way up to Atlanta to satisfy his latest contract. He loved the way his silver Chevy Silverado hugged the road, and he was glad he'd upgraded and sold the Blazer that had once been his pride and joy.

* * *

Real's phone had been buzzing all day with calls from his ever-growing base of clientele, looking to spend on his new product. The heroin was brining in far more money than the cocaine he'd once sold. He knew he'd be back on top in no time.

Headed down Northside Drive to Fair Street to pick up the money for his last drop-off, Real smiled to himself. As he passed the Georgia Dome, he thought back on the last game he'd attended with Constance. She had cried as the New Orleans Saints kicked the winning field goal, knocking the Falcons out of the playoffs.

Pulling up at the liquor store on the corner of Fair Street and Northside Drive, Real got out and waited for Savage to show up with the remaining $17,000 he owed on his last drop. Real sat and watched the neighborhood crack-heads and alcoholics begging for money in the parking lot. He shook his head, pitying the road some people's lives had taken.

After thirty minutes passed and there was still no sign of Savage, Real gave him a call. It rang three times and then went to voicemail. Real tried his best to keep thinking positive, but after an hour had passed, his blood began to boil. "I just know this fuck nigga ain't trying me," Real whispered to himself as he turned the ignition key, bringing the truck to life.

Real hit the gas, burning rubber as he sped angrily out of the lot, en route to Savage's trap house. After Real bent around a couple of blocks, Savage's old, run-down, wood-framed house came into view. As Real got closer, he saw three customized Chevies in the yard; one of them belonged to Savage. He whipped up behind the cars, killed the truck engine, grabbed his favorite piece—his Glock .40—and exited the truck with attitude. He stepped up on the porch and looked through the screen door, which was barely hanging on its hinges just like Savage was gonna barely be holding on to his pulse if he didn't pay up.

"Seven-eleven, nigga! Tighten up, nigga! Scared money don't make no money!" one of the unfamiliar men called out.

Savage positioned himself on one knee, sweating out of control, throwing the dice in the circle of men that had beaten him out of most of the $17,000 he owed Real. He was a gambler at heart, so when Bell, Great, Rod, and Chase came through talking about a game of craps, he figured it would be a quick way to double his money.

What the careless, betting fool didn't know was that every since he'd discovered newfound wealth, his circle of friends had been plotting against him. They'd seen their so-called patna go from making a couple hundred to a couple thousand a day, and Savage wasn't spreading his wealth around to the rest of his crew. They knew how Savage loved to gamble, so they put a plan together to beat him out of the money he was stacking. Their plan had worked, Savage only had a measly $1,300 left out of the $17,000 he'd started with; he had gambled Real's money away with a few rolls of the dice.

Savage was more of a killer than a hustler, but Real had still entrusted him to handle the trap. Savage knew how to get the money; his problem was that he had no idea how to *keep* it.

Real stood in the doorway and just watched for a minute before he made his move. He faulted himself for going back to his old 'hood and trying to help one of his old trap buddies. Real watched as the four men gave each other satisfied looks behind the short, stubby Savage's back while he crapped out and lost every dime he had— dimes that didn't even technically belong to him because he still owed Real a nice chunk of cash.

"Fuck!" Savage screamed as the five and two showed

on the dice.

"Boy, put down. You can keep shooting," Chase called out as Savage stood and wiped the sweat from his brow.

"Man, I'm out, but hold up. Can y'all just front me $5,000 to go back? I'll have it to you by tonight if I lose," he said to the stocky, light-skinned Great, the pretty boy hustler of the crew.

"Nigga, how I look gambling against my own money? I gotta catch up with this li'l broad anyway. I'll catch y'all later," Great said proudly as he started stuffing his winnings in his pockets.

Real knew when he went in that he would have to shoot off the rip, because the men in the house were most likely strapped. Gripping the Glock tightly he pushed the screen door open and stepped in.

Pop! Pop!

"Ahhh!" Chase screamed, holding his leg as Real stood in the doorway with his gun aimed at the crew.

"All y'all niggas lay down!" Real screamed, ready to unload on anybody who made a false move.

"Who you? Player, you fucking up!" Rod spat before the Glock .40 bullet hit him in the shoulder, followed by one hitting him in the stomach, causing him to double over and drop to the floor.

"Anybody else got somethin' to say?" Real screamed out as he walked over to Savage, who was lying on the floor, shaking.

"Look, Real, man, I had your bread, but I thought I could fl—"

Savage was cut off as Bell jumped up and tried to run,

but the Glock cut him down, hitting him twice in the back and sending him face first to the floor.

"Nigga, I oughtta kill you right here and now!" Real screamed at Savage, pissed that he had to put in all that unnecessary work to get the money that was rightfully his. As he surveyed the scene and saw the blood puddles grow thicker, Real knew he needed to head out in a hurry. "Nigga, get up and get my money from these fools!" Real yelled at Savage.

Savage jumped up instantly and started going through his crew's pocket, grabbing all the money he could find. Minutes later, all the blood-soaked cash was sitting on the old wooden coffee table. "That's it, Real," Savage said, looking on helplessly as his crew squirmed in pain from the gunshot wounds.

"Nigga, you a real bitch!" Real screamed as he lifted the Glock to Savages face and pulled the trigger, knocking him backward, right off his feet.

After getting all his money and then some, Real exited the house, jumped in the truck, and headed home, still pissed that he had to put in so much work for his own damn money.

Just as Real was pulling into his complex, a Chevy Silverado circled the apartments, looking for Apartment 36. Blanco couldn't wait to make is grand entrance and introduce himself to his next victim right before he took the man's life.

Chapter 26

Real sat in the kitchen and counted all the money from the day's pick-ups. It came out to $140,000, good for a slow week. He gathered up all the stacks and bagged them up before he went to take a shower. As he lathered up, he thought about how things were about to be for him. The money was coming in, and he knew things were about to be like old times for him. "I'm doin' it, baby," he said to an imaginary Constance as the soapy water ran down the drain. "Your boy's getting' back on top!"

Blanco waited until the sun had completely disappeared behind the horizon before he made his move. He pulled up outside of Real's neighbor's apartment and selected his knife of choice, then pulled on his gloves and exited the truck. He walked up to the door and tried the knob, but it was locked. He stood on his tiptoes to look in the front window, but he didn't see anyone. Looking around to make sure the coast was clear, he walked to the left, headed to the back of the apartment. He stepped up on the back stoop of Real's apartment and peeked into the tall sliding-glass doors; he still saw no movement whatsoever. He then made his way over to the back bathroom window. When he looked inside through the steamy window, he saw the silhouette of a man moving around behind the shower curtain. He knew it was more than likely Real, his target, so he planned to take advantage of the running shower; he could pick the lock on the front door without being heard.

Just as Blanco turned to head back to the front door, a uniformed man with a flashlight ordered him to freeze. "Don't move, mister!" screamed the petite, clearly inexperienced white boy, who'd only been working apartment security for a whopping two weeks.

Blanco's heart dropped as the man appeared out of nowhere. "Uh, I'm sorry, sir. I lost my dog. I need help," he said, sounding stressed as he pretended to look for his lost dog while trying his best to conceal the long blade in his hand. "Rover! Here, Rover!" he called, whistling and frantically looking around. He even almost faked a tear, which was a stretch since the man didn't have a compassionate bone in his body.

"Freeze!" the young white apartment security guard repeated, taking notice of the shiny blade Blanco was trying to hide from him.

"I'm only looking for Rover!" Blanco screamed as he lifted the knife and pounced on the man.

The young security guard was totally shocked by Blanco's sudden display of aggression. "Hey! Mister, stop! Ah!" He groaned, trying his best to get away from the blade as Blanco slashed and stabbed until the man broke down and stopped moving.

Pissed that his attack on Real had been interrupted, Blanco rushed back out to his truck and sped away from the scene just in case someone had heard something and called the police. Blanco shouted and cursed while riding down Washington Road, headed back to his hotel room. He was pissed that he'd have to spend yet another night in Atlanta. Before he got to his hotel, he changed his mind and whipped the truck around.

* * *

Real finished bathing and found a good spot on the couch to relax and watch a game. Before he knew it, he was nodding off, having no idea that the man who'd killed his baby—the very man he was hunting—had just committed another murder right outside his back door.

Real was sound asleep and didn't hear a thing as the police and GBI scoured the scene around the dead security guard. His neighbor Groundhog had noticed the man while he was putting his trash out and had quickly called the police.

The knock at the door in the middle of the night startled Real, and he was even more shocked to look out the peephole and see police everywhere. "Fuck! I knew it!" Real called out. He rushed to the back of the apartment, grabbed his pistol, and positioned himself in a corner. He decided that he'd have his gun blazing when they came in, because he refused to go back to prison.

He'd already decided that if it ever came down to being locked up again, he'd have his court trial in the streets. Now, positioned in a corner and thinking there was a raid on his place, he gripped the gun tight and was ready to shoot.

After a couple more unanswered knocks, the detective and the two uniformed officers turned and went to the other apartments to see if they could get any leads on the murder.

Real's heart raced as he waited and waited. Twenty minutes later, after the knocks had stopped, Real lifted up and tiptoed over to the window and peeked out. He saw the police cars and the ambulance leaving. There were a few suits talking to people who lived in the complex. Real breathed a sigh of relief, but when he turned, he faced a short little white man, standing in the middle of the room, smiling and holding a huge knife. "Who the fuck—"

Blanco was on him before he could get the question fully out of his mouth. The knife cut through the fabric of Real's shirt and made a big gash across his arm with ease.

Real fought off the little strong man the best he could, but Blanco sliced and stabbed Real repeatedly until all his clothes were soaked in blood. Real felt himself getting weak from blood loss and pain, but he knew if he quit fighting, the small man would no doubt hit his target and kill him. Real back-peddled a bit, trying his best to fend off the man who kept swinging the knife at his face.

"Don't run, you fuckin' coward! Come on! Fight like a man! I think I'll tell Angelo this one's on the house since you're so damn easy to kill. Shit, your slutty little girlfriend put up more of a fight than you," Blanco spat as he kept slicing at a dodging Real.

"You? You killed my lady?" Real called out, trying his best to escape the brutal blade. The mention of Constance's death took Real to another place. He knew he was now facing the man who had taken everything from him, the man who'd killed his baby girl. "Ahh!" Real screamed out as the knife caught him in the side. He knew he'd be out before long, because he'd lost too much blood to go on. He looked over and saw the 9mm that he'd placed on the side of the bed when he'd thought the police were about to kick in the door. Real turned away from the charging attack and sacrificed his back to the knife just so he could get to the gun.

"You're nothing but a fuckin' coward! I'm gonna slaughter you like I did your bitch!" Blanco said. He caught Real in the back twice before he could get to the gun.

Real dived for the gun, and as soon as it was in hands, he turned to destroy his attacker, his lover's murderer.

By that time, Blanco saw what was going down. He turned to retreat, but it was too late.

Real pulled the trigger, catching him in the leg and hip, the hollow-point bullets sending him instantly crashing to the floor.

"Uh! Goddamn it!" Blanco screamed out in pain, dropping the knife as he tried to crawl away.

Real saw him hit the ground. He dragged his bloody self over to the wounded Blanco as Blanco tried to use his upper body strength to pull himself out of harm's way. When Real got close enough, he grabbed Blanco's ankle and pulled himself on top of the helpless small man. "Where ya big knife now, you little bitch?" Real said forcefully as his body weight stopped Blanco in his tracks. Real used all of his energy to flip Blanco on his back as the little man tried his best to fight Real off. Once he was perched on top of Blanco, Real shoved the big pistol into the man's little mouth.

"Ah!" Blanco began to scream, but he was silenced as the gun touched his tonsils.

Real pushed the gun hard into his mouth, trying to choke the life out of him.

Blanco's eyes grew huge with fear as the gun cut off his breathing.

"You li'l bitch!" Real screamed as he pulled the trigger, sending the bullet traveling through Blanco's throat and out the back of his scrawny little neck.

Real's gun was covered with blood and other throat matter. He rolled off Blanco and crawled over to the phone. Instead of 911 he dialed Kelly, his old-school partner Dooby's sister. As the nurse for his crew, Kelly had treated gunshot wounds, stab wounds, and severe beatings. She and Real were cool, and she always used to tell Real that in the business he was in, he would need her one day. He'd laughed it off before, but now, after all those years, she would finally be right about that.

Chapter 27

The next day, B-Low sat in the stained glass cubicle with Walter Pendleton, one of Atlanta's most accomplished high-profile lawyers. Pendleton had shot to prominence when he'd successfully defended Dexter Grant, a highly recognized NBA talent who'd been charged with killing his live-in girlfriend. The media had tried to convict Dexter with bad press even before the jury had been selected, and Walter knew the killing of Sandy Kilgore, the young white granddaughter of Congressman Theodore Kilgore, would be an uphill battle from start to finish. Everyone had counted Dexter out, especially with all the evidence that had been stacked up against him. Just when the D.A. thought he had a win under his belt, Walter produced a piece of evidence, complemented by a story good enough for a Hollywood script. The jury fell for it, hands down. When the "not guilty" verdict was read, Walter had smiled and made sure he got in the lens of every camera and in the mic of every reporter covering the high-profile case. Later that evening, he collected the extra two million from Dexter and met with each one of the jurors he had paid off for their cooperation. Walter didn't care how he won a case. His motto was, "A win is a win, no matter how you get it." The Dexter Grant case and all the ones that had followed had made him an overnight legal sensation. He was 9-0 for those who were keeping score, and the press considered Walter a genius. What they didn't know was that he had connections in both high and low places.

"What you mean, man? How long am I going to have to sit in this muthafucker?" B-Low asked as Walter explained to him that in his case, a bond would be highly unlikely. "Man, no bond?" B-Low screamed, making Walter jump.

"We aren't going to count out the bond just yet, but I have to tell you it will be a long shot. On my way back down, I'll speak with the D.A., and later tonight I'll contact the attorney general to see what we're up against."

"Look, Walter, I've got a business to run. I can't be locked up in here," B-Low stressed, looking disheveled and still wearing the clothes from the day before.

"I totally agree. Look, sometimes we get dealt a bad hand. As you know, when that happens, we've got to play it like a champ. I specialize in making something out of nothing. The conspiracy, money-laundering, and tax evasion charges they're holding you on can be beaten, especially without any illegal substance to back up their claims. Just be patient and let me look into everything. I'll come up with the best defense to beat this case and get you out of here ASAP," Walter said as he glanced over B-Low's arrest reports.

"I appreciate that, but be straight with me. How long am I going to have to be here if I don't get a bond?" B-Low asked, thinking about the whipping he'd taken from the young kid in the holding cell. He leaned forward and whispered to his attorney, "Some of these fuckas is crazy in here!"

"If you don't get a bond, you could be here for three to five months before we get you to trial," Walter told B-Low as he slid the paperwork into his signature Gucci briefcase and put on his solid gold-rimmed Ralph Lauren frames.

"Mannnn! I'm spending too much money to be sitting up in this bitch for that long! Is there any kind of way we can make it sooner? Like I told you, I've got a damn business to run," B-Low spat, jumping up out of his chair and causing it to tip. He paced the small, cramped room like a caged animal.

"Look, man, let me be honest with you, Low. These people in the so-called justice system don't give a fuck about your business, your mother, or your fucking dog! All they care about is getting your ass on a platter. If you want me to get your ass off that platter and back to your business and whatever else you've got going on, you're going to have to be fucking patient. Right now, you're going to have to lie back and chill the fuck out while I do my job! You paid me close to a million to save your ass, and that's what I'm going to do, but you've got to give me time to go through the proper channels," Walter snapped.

He adjusted his expensive silk tie and stood to leave.

B-Low was shocked to hear the old distinguished, gray-haired white man speak in such a heated manner, but he hung on to every word. "My bad, man. This shit's just fucked up," B-Low mumbled as he stuck his hand out to Walter.

"As you and I know, when you play in the streets, you have to pay your dues. It's your time to pay, but we just don't want you paying too much," Walter told B-Low as he knocked on the glass and signaled for the officer to let him out.

B-Low stood speechless as he watched Walter step onto the elevator and press the ground floor button. Seconds later, the doors closed.

"Come on," the female jailer called out to B-Low, who had his back turned to her, lost in deep thought. A few minutes later, she was closing the Pod 1 door, locking B-Low into the place where he would spend months, awaiting trial.

Chapter 28

Kelly rushed over to Real's spot as soon as she hung up the phone. She could tell by his voice as he gave her his address that he was hurt pretty badly. "Real! Real!" she screamed as she knelt beside him, trying her best not to look at the gruesome sight of what was left of Blanco. After checking Real's pulse, she got up and ran back to the front to lock the door. She didn't need any special visitors or the police rushing up in the spot with a dead man lying there.

She saw that Real had already lost a lot of blood, so she dumped the contents of her medical bag out on the floor next to him and grabbed what she needed to stop the bleeding. She picked up the surgical scissors and began carefully cutting all of Real's clothes off. She was surprised to see so many bleeding wounds, clearly gashes that had been made by the knife lying next to the dead man. Just when she thought she'd cleaned up the last wound, she came across another one. She stitched up every knife entry point. "Damn it!" she cursed under her breath as she moved to the next gash.

An hour later, Real started to come to.

Kelly wiped his completely naked body down with alcohol and peroxide as he lay still. She took in his sculptured physique and enjoyed every minute of the wipe-down.

Just as she was about finished, his eyes came open.

"What the hell happened here, Real?" she asked as her eyes darted to the nearly decapitated corpse beside them.

"Ah! Damn! Shit," Real moaned out in pain as he tried to get up off the floor.

"No, just lie there for a minute and be still. Don't get up," she instructed, laying her perfectly manicured hand on his chest and gently pushing him back down.

"Look, we go to get up out of here. Ah!" Real said, trying his best to stay steady as Kelly started wiping him down again with the alcohol-drenched cloth to get the rest of the blood off him. Real noticed that his manhood was hardening, so he tried to lay his hand awkwardly over it.

"No need. I already saw it. I wiped it down too," Kelly said, smiling. There were times when she truly loved her job. She remembered back when she'd first met Real, back when he and her brother used to do a lot of business. She had been instantly attracted to the tall, dark-skinned brother. The second time meeting him was in her brother's pool room, when a masked man had come in to rob the place. That man ended up dead, and her brother's li'l protégé ended up with a bullet in his leg. Kelly was called in to repair the damage. She'd given Real her info that night, and they'd been in touch periodically every since, especially after Dooby's death.

Real was glad that after all those years, her number hadn't changed. "Oh yeah?" Real said looking up at the oval-faced, caramel-complexioned Kelly. She was kind of thin for his taste, but her beauty compensated for her size.

"Yeah, really. Look, you need to go somewhere so you can get some rest. Matter fact, you're coming home with me, no ifs, ands, or buts about it. Come on," she said as she placed her hands under Real and pulled him up to his feet.

"Ah! Oh! Ah!" Real screamed out in pain as he stood and limped off with Kelly's help. He made sure to kick and spit on Blanco on the way out. "Li'l bitch," Real muttered as Kelly acted as his crutch all the way out to her car. "Wait," he said, "I can't leave my truck." Real pulled away from her and limped over to his Dodge, but then he realized he didn't have his keys.

"Uh, are you sure you can drive?"

"Yeah, I'll be a'ight. I'm good."

"Okay. I'll get the keys. Where they at?"

"In the kitchen, on the table," Real said as he slowly climbed behind the wheel of his truck.

Minutes later, Kelly was handing Real his keys and giving him her address just in case they got separated in traffic. "Let's roll," she told Real as she turned and got in her car.

Real followed her out to Peachtree City, where she had a spacious two-bedroom condo. He decided on his way out to her spot that he was going to lie low for a minute and then head to Miami.

Chapter 29

Angelo sat back in his beach house with Christie, his on-again/off-again girlfriend. He looked at his watch, baffled as to why Blanco hadn't checked in yet. In fact, he hadn't heard from the little hit man since he'd called the hit in on Real. Still, he was confident that Blanco would get the job done and contact him soon regarding the remainder of his pay.

"What's wrong, suga lump? Why the sad face?" Christie asked Angelo as she walked over and stood next to him on the balcony that jutted out over a 100-foot cliff above a roaring river and a jagged cluster of rocks. The view out on the balcony was beautiful, like something straight out of a photographer's portfolio.

"I'm okay. I've just got a lot on my mind. Every since Mike was killed by Milo, there's been a lot of tension between the families. They think somebody else was involved in the hit. There's just a lot of BS going on," Angelo said as they stood side by side, watching the water beat the rocks below.

The mention of Milo's name brought a sad scowl over Christie's face that Angelo noticed, though he didn't comment on it. "Everything is gonna be okay, baby. Come here. Let me make you feel better," she said, wrapping her arms around his waist while kissing him softly on the neck.

Angelo thought about everything that had been going on within the families. He knew it was only going to get worse. Since he'd taken over as head of the family, he had been the go-to man with the cartel. He now realized just how much his uncle had on his plate. A lot of what his uncle had done had kept the cartel intact and financially stable. His uncle had been a vital part of the livelihood of the entire organization. Now, since he'd been chosen to take his uncle's place, the families expected him to fulfill his uncle's duties, and that was stressing him out like crazy.

Even after cutting Milo down like he deserved, Angelo still didn't feel vindicated or satisfied. Truth be told, he was entirely fed up with his involvement in the circle of families. He was burnt out, and he wanted out, but he knew leaving the ranks would mean an automatic death sentence. The stress of the job that he held within the family was getting the best of him, and Christie seemed to only make the situation worse. She was getting on the few remaining nerves he had. "Sure. Come make me feel better," Angelo said as she unzipped his pants and pulled out his limp member.

Christie followed his lead and knelt before him. She

wrapped her thick lips around his growing erection.

"Ah yeah," Angelo moaned as sinister thoughts ran through his head. After a few minutes of sucking, he hoisted Christie up on the balcony rail and pulled up her skirt. His entry was real easy, being that she wasn't wearing any panties under her sundress and was already dripping wet with desire.

"Ohhhh, baaabyyyyy!" she moaned as he entered her roughly while she wrapped her legs around him.

"Yeah! Oh shit, yes! Ahh!" Angelo moaned, remembering how Milo used to have Christie in the same position back at his place.

"Fuck this pussy, babyyyy! Damn, I love your cock!" Christie screamed as she wildly thrust her hips against him, trying to get all of him into her.

"Yeah! Oh yeah, bitch! You think I don't know about you and Milo?" Angelo screamed as he grabbed her tight and jammed himself inside of her roughly.

"What? Wh-what are you—"

"Ah!" Angelo moaned as he emptied himself inside of a confused and scared Christie.

Christie and Milo had been seeing each other behind Angelo's back for quite some time, while Milo was still alive. Angelo hadn't been sure at first, and he was naïve in thinking neither of them would dare betray him like that, so he'd dismissed the signs he picked up on whenever they were all in each other's presence. It was at his birthday party that he was convinced otherwise. The looks Milo and Christie had given each other during the party, looks that they thought went unnoticed, were all the proof Angelo needed to put Howard Bell, his personal private eye, on the job.

A week later, Howard showed up at Angelo's restaurant and laid out a stack of pictures of Christie and Milo together. The ones that really hurt Angelo were the close-ups of Milo and Christie out on Milo's balcony, having sex in various positions.

The hate Angelo had already harbored had doubled after seeing those pictures; it was yet another reason Angelo took such pleasure in pumping the bullets into the disloyal, backstabbing Milo the day he'd tried to flee the wrath of the cartel. Angelo would never forget the shocked, confused expression on Milo's face as he fell to the ground. He cherished that memory already.

"Angelo, what are you saying?" she asked as she tried to hop off the ledge of the balcony.

"You know exactly what I'm saying, you whore. You ain't nothing but a lying piece of shit. Fuck you," Angelo said calmly. He quickly bent down and grabbed both of her legs and flipped her off of the balcony, sending her flailing helplessly down into the speared rocks and cascading water.

"Noooooo!" Christie screamed as she flipped through the air and crashed into a cluster of sharp rocks that broke her bones and pierced her body.

When Angelo looked down and couldn't see any sign of her, he grabbed his binoculars that he kept on his balcony for bird-watching and focused in on the area where she'd fallen. He caught a glimpse of her just as the current dragged her away through the rough rapids.

Angelo walked back into his place and made a call to his yacht captain. He had decided to leave the cartel, he'd gotten rid of the cheating whore, and now he was now ready to live a normal life. He'd already been making plans to disappear on his yacht, and his trusty captain would play a major role in those plans. He hoped everyone would believe he'd fallen off the boat. But before he faked his death to avoid suffering a real one, he had to make sure Blanco had handled the business with the man named Real, the man who had killed his uncle.

G STREET CHRONICLES
A NEW URBAN DYNASTY

WWW.GSTREETCHRONICLES.COM

Chapter 30

A Week Later...

B-Low was sitting in his cell doing a crossword puzzle when his name was called.

"Lawyer visit!" the jailer called out from the front of the pod, patiently waiting to escort B-Low out to the small glass room to see his attorney.

B-Low was already seated when Walter walked in and sat across from him at the cheap wooden table that the state provided for lawyer/ inmate visits. Without saying a word, Walter pulled a file marked "Urgent" out if his briefcase and laid it on the table.

B-Low looked on curiously, knowing something was undoubtedly wrong.

"Check that out," Walter said, breaking the silence as he removed his frames and pinched the bridge of his nose, trying to calm down the migraine that he felt coming on.

"Hold the fuck up! I ain't believing this shit, man!

They killed Grump, and now Kap and Yella pushing this nigga's murder on me when I don't even know him?" B-Low choked out as his heart raced. "This some shit, man! Some straight-up bullshit!"

"Let me give you the whole rundown. The FBI went to round up your crew. As they rushed the location, a shoot-out ensued. Your friend Grump was killed, and the other two were brought in for questioning. Turns out you were the main topic of their interrogation, so after the smoke cleared and Kap and Yella were charged with murder, facing a possible life sentence, they both started flapping their lips. Kap put you at the scene of an old murder, one he claimed you've bragged about on several occasions. They both ratted you out. Evidently, the police believe your so-called friends, so that's the reason why you have a murder charge hanging over your head now," Walter explained, rearing back in his chair.

"Murder? Oh hell naw!" B-Low screamed.

When Low slammed his fist violently down on the table, the noise caused the jailers to rush into the room. "What's going on in here? Is everything okay, sir?" they asked Walter, looking back and forth between the accused and the attorney.

"Yes, Officers. Everything is just fine. He's just a little emotional. Thank you for checking in on us, gentlemen," Walter told them and then waited for the door to close before he spoke again. "Look, I met with my people yesterday. Your federal charges can disappear for a generous amount, but this murder charge is a whole different animal. Your crew members laying the blame on you doesn't make it any better, but at least we won't have to fight the feds on this one. It's far easier to deal with the state," Walter told B-Low, who stared at the statements with a blank look on his face.

"This is... Man, I ain't killed nobody," B-Low lied, reflecting back on Quad, lying lifeless in the street. He leaned back in his chair and cupped his face with his hands.

"I think I can get the D.A. to work with you. I think the best thing for us to do is to go after a plea on this one, since your friends are fingering you. Besides, we need to keep quiet so the deal I made to get rid of the federal charges doesn't come up. People's careers will be at risk if the shuffling of paperwork is discovered. If we push this thing to trial, all our skeletons are going to come out of the closet, leaving the alphabet boys plenty of room to nail your ass to the cross. Really, the best thing to do is to shoot for a deal. I'll make some calls tonight and see what I can work out."

"Plea? Man, look, I—"

"Low, we don't have a choice right now, unless you want your old federal charges to reappear while you're trying to fight the state case for the murder," Walter fired back, not letting him finish. "You have to strike a deal, or things are going to be much worse."

"Man, what kind of time we talking?" B-Low asked weakly, knowing he had no choice.

"I'm going to push for ten, but they may try to counter with fifteen. It all depends on how much you plan on spending."

"How much I'll spend? What you talking about?" B-Low asked, confused.

"Money talks. You know that. You need to pay me a retainer for this charge. I called in a favor to clear the federal charges, but now you've got state charges to deal with. My retainer is $250,000, and if you want to shoot for the ten years, you'd better let your money do the talking," Walter told him as he reached over, grabbed the file, and placed it back in his briefcase.

"How 'bout $250,000 both ways? That's a half-million. That should be more than enough to cover your retainer *and* get the ten years," B-Low said, still trying to stomach the fact that he was going to have to do some time no matter what.

"Hmm. I think that just might do the job. Can you get your people to meet me?" Walter asked. He knew he could easily get the ten years for a mere $5,000, being that he and the D.A. were fishing buddies, but he was happy to make a profit.

"Yeah, no problem."

"Same number, same place?" Walter asked.

"Yeah. I'll call Nikki and let her know what's up," B-Low replied, thanking God that Nikki, the only female in his crew, had kept it real.

"Okay. That will be great. I will wait for the call from your associate. In the meantime, take it easy," Walter told B-Low. Then he gathered all of his belongings, put his glasses back on, and exited the room.

After being escorted back to the pod, B-Low rushed over to the wall phone and called Nikki. "Girl, you good?

What the fuck happened?" B-Low asked forcefully, pissed at his crew's back-stabbing ways.

"B-Low, I'm so glad you called. The feds kicked in the spot four nights ago. Grump started blasting. When it was all said and done, he lay dead, and everybody else was locked up. Kap and Yella called me yesterday to tell me they had bonds for $50,000 a piece, but you know I wouldn't touch your money till your say so. They can bounce with that though," Nikki explained as she sat in her humble one-bedroom apartment on the outskirts of Atlanta, hoping her name wouldn't come up in the midst of all the investigations.

"Look, Nikki, my lawyer just showed me statements from both of them niggas, pointing the finger at me shit. That's probably why they got bonds! I read everything them niggas said straight up," B-Low spat with a scowl plastered across his face.

"What? Oh hell naw, B!" Nikki shouted, trying her best to sound surprised and pissed at the same time at the disloyalty within the crew.

"Bond 'em out one by one and slump 'em," B-Low said, calmly and coolly.

"I can't believe them niggas, B, but you know it's done. Death before dishonor all day over here," Nikki called out as she eyed her .45 automatic resting on her nightstand.

"Oh, and another thang. You need to call Walter, my lawyer. Meet him with a half-mill. I'll explain the rest to you later."

"A half-mill? Really?"

"Yep."

"Okay. I'll hit him right now. Love you, man." She hung up the phone with B-Low and looked over at Kap, who had just gotten out of the shower and was applying lotion to his lean, ripped body. "And I love you too," she said.

"What that fool talking about?" he asked as he walked over and kissed her softly on the lips.

"He told me to take you and Yella out…oh, and to give his lawyer half a million." She laughed.

"Oh yeah? That's why his dumb ass gonna be sitting still for a long time. We supposed to been moved on his ass. I just hate I got to face this murder charge, but as long as Yella is taken care of, we good," Kap said as Nikki grabbed the lotion from him and applied some to his back.

"I'm gonna bond him out today and take care of him. You need to just make sure you in your lawyer office when shit go down, because you'll need an alibi when they look your way," Nikki told him while gently running her perfectly manicured nails down his back and going over her plans in her head.

"See? That's why I love my baby. You're always thinking ahead. Grab $50,000 from that bag for the bond and go ahead and put the rest in my car. As soon as I leave this lawyer's office we heading out to Houston. We'll hole up there till I gotta come back for trial," Kap told her as he got dressed. "Ain't nobody gonna mess with us in Texas, baby."

"Okay. I'll meet you out at the Burger King on North-side Drive at 5 o'clock. Yella will be taken care of by then," she said assuredly, excited about the trip she and Kap were about to take. She took the bag that contained more than two million outside and tucked it behind the seat on the back floor of Kap's 750 BMW.

"That'll work," Kap said to himself as he exited the apartment minutes behind her. "A'ight, boo, handle your business and be careful," Kap told her as he climbed behind the wheel of his 750 BMW and brought the engine to life.

"I will, baby. See you at 5:00," Nikki told him as she thought about his seed that was growing inside of her.

Nikki and Kap had been messing around on the side, unbeknownst to the crew, for a long time. They'd also been devising a plan to take out B-Low, but just as they were about to put it in action, the feds had come down on them. A couple days later, the police had raided the spot, and Yella and Kap were arrested. Kap convinced Yella to turn on B-Low, and they put a plot together to put everything on him. After talking to detectives and making statements, they were offered bonds in exchange for their cooperation. Nikki had come to Kap's rescue in no time, and Kap had promised Yella he'd be back for him the next day. Kap knew he had to stay around Yella until the trial so his story wouldn't change, but Nikki had a better plan: They'd just get rid of him altogether.

G STREET CHRONICLES
~A NEW URBAN DYNASTY~

WWW.GSTREETCHRONICLES.COM

Chapter 31

*K*elly nursed Real back to good health in no time, and he was now back to his morning workouts and handling business.

"You know, I really appreciate everything you've done for me. You saved my life," Real told her as he packed up the things Kelly had purchased for him during his recuperation.

"You can stay here as long as you like," she told Real as she stood in the doorway of the guest room wearing nothing but a sheer satin nightgown that left nothing to the imagination.

"I'll be back as soon as I take care of this unfinished business in Miami," Real said, trying hard not to look. She was his old friend's sister, and he was trying hard to show some respect.

"Okay, cool. I always got your back, Real," Kelly promised him as she walked over and gave him a hug, pressing firmly against him.

It was getting harder by the day for Real not to give in to Kelly's advances, and he knew if he didn't get out of her spot soon, they'd end up in bed together.

Real stepped out to his truck and grabbed a backpack from the passenger seat. It was filled with money. He withdrew $10,000 and tucked it into the glove compartment, then took the backpack inside. "Hold this down for me. Spend whatever you need. I'll be back soon," Real said, handing her the bag with just over a quarter-million in it.

"I got you, Real...and thanks," she said as she moved in for another hug.

"No, thank *you*, Kelly. You saved my life," Real said as he held her in his arms.

Out of nowhere, she palmed the back of Real's head and pulled him down to her, kissing him deeply while slowly grinding her hips into him.

A minute later, they loosened their embrace, and Real turned and walked out without another word.

Kelly stood in the doorway watching him until he turned the corner and was out of sight.

Real pushed the truck down Highway 85 south, en route to the place where it had all begun years ago: Miami. Ten hours later, he contacted his old Miami connect, Sergio. After all that time, Real was surprised that Sergio was still in business.

"Hello?"

"Yo, Sergio!"

"Yeah? Who speakin'?" Sergio asked curiously.

"Real—the one and only," Real replied jokingly.

"Not the man himself! Real! How's it going, man?"

"Good. Look, Serg, I need some help. I'll be in your neck of the woods in less than an hour. I need information on my old friend Angelo," Real said firmly.

"Angelo? Moretti's nephew? Come on now, Real. Not again," Sergio grumbled. He wanted nothing to do with the murder of another member of one of the most powerful cartel-backed families in the South.

"I need an address, Sergio," Real told him, dismissing the reluctance in his voice.

Sergio thought about the investigation that had come behind the last massacres. He vividly remembered sitting with Angelo and a couple other high-up cartel members at a social gathering for a local politician. They'd all sat around with the crooked members of the police force and FBI. Angelo had promised them a generous amount of money to find out who had passed any information to the man named Real because he knew only someone close to the families could have known where they resided. Sergio's stomach had boiled and his heart raced when the FBI agent assured Angelo that he could find out without a doubt. Only months later was Sergio able to breathe easy again, and now Real was throwing him right back into that uneasy situation. Times were hard for Sergio, though, so he decided to take a chance and get Real the info. "Look, Real, this time it's going to be a bit more," Sergio said weakly. "It's a huge risk on my end. There are a lot of big players involved, listening and watching very closely."

"Okay. Just let me know your price when you call me

back with the information," Real told him, willing to pay whatever the cost.

"I'll do it for $20,000, and you can meet me at the Royal Palm Hotel on MLK, Room 303," Sergio blurted out.

"Twenty?" Real sighed, none too happy that his old friend was clearly trying to take advantage of him.. "Okay, cool. I'll be there in less than an hour." He punched the location into his GPS, and it alerted him that he was thirty miles away from the destination. Forty-five minutes later, Real was parking the truck in the hotel parking lot and heading up to Room 303.

Before he could knock, Sergio pulled the door open and let him in. "Real! It's good to see ya," Sergio called out, gently slapping Real on the shoulder. He nudged him inside and pushed the door closed.

"Yeah. Well? What you got for me? Any good news?" Real asked in a very serious tone as he walked over and stood in the middle of the room.

"Yeah. I've got an address and a slew of other info that might help you, but, uh…well, like I told you, it'll be $20,000 this time. From the looks of you, my friend, it won't hurt you a bit," Sergio said, looking Real up and down playfully as he walked over and grabbed the small yellow pad that contained all the information he could find on Angelo.

Just as Sergio turned around, a loud *Bang*! shook the room. Seconds later, he placed his hand over the stinging hole in his chest. When he pulled it away and looked at it, he saw that it was full of blood.

Real walked over to him and snatched the pad from his free hand. He lifted the gun again and sent another bullet through his old friend's chest, right into his heart.

Sergio crumbled to the floor, lifeless, with a look of surprise on his face.

Real tore the page with Angelo's info from the pad and stuck his head out the door. Seeing that the coast was clear, he stepped out of the room and jumped into his truck to head to the address Sergio had jotted down on the piece of paper.

Chapter 32

Kap was on his way to see his lawyer while Nikki was en route to pick Yella up from the Fulton County Jail. Kap had devised the ultimate plan, and he knew just the lawyer to help him pull it all off. He had put more than half of B-Low's cash in the lawyer's pocket, and he knew the last payment would keep him free.

Thirty minutes later, he was pulling into the lawyer's parking lot. Before he exited the car, he called Nikki. "Hey, baby. Where you at?" Kap asked as he watched a perfectly tan blonde exit the office and get into a cherry-red convertible Aston-Martin.

"Up the street from the jail. You sure the stash house is open?"

"Wide open and empty. Just make sure you call me as soon as you get him in the car," Kap told her, thinking about the remaining bricks of cocaine he'd taken from the house and secretly stashed in his Aunt Lydia's spot out in Decatur.

"I will, baby."

"Okay. Love you."

"Love you too."

Kap ended the call and headed into the lawyer's office with the extra cash for the lawyer to, as he put it, "rub a few palms." Kap knew the million would rub more than a few palms, but he didn't care about the cost, as long as he remained free. Besides, the money was compliments of B-Low.

"Hi. Do you have an appointment?" the young, perky, *Playboy* bunny-looking white girl asked as Kap walked through the door and approached her desk.

"Yeah, uh, could you—"

"It's all right, Heather," a distinguished-looking older white male called out from the back office doorway. "Come on back," he said, motioning Kap to his office.

As Kap made his way to the back, he took in all of the expensive furnishings and portraits that lined the walls of the spacious office building. In the back office, he was in awe of the expensive cherry-oak custom furnishings with gold accents.

"You got the money?" the lawyer asked bluntly as he took a seat in his high-backed soft leather desk chair.

"Yeah, but I need to know if you have the deal in place or not," Kap shot back, holding the money out in front of him.

"Mr. Pendleton, you have a call on Line 1!" the receptionist announced over his office intercom.

"Take a message, Heather, and make sure you get the number," he replied. He reached over and flipped off the intercom switch, then leaned in and grabbed the bag of money.

"Look, it's all there. I gave you what you asked for, so I expect B-Low to sign off on that plea. If he don't, my ass is going down with him, and we ain't gonna like that, are we, Walter?" Kap said firmly, making sure the attorney would pick up on his subtle threat.

"Don't worry. I'll get him to take the plea and admit to the murder, so you'll be fully exonerated. I've already talked to the D.A. As soon as the papers are signed, your case is out the door," Walter said in a tough tone, trying his best not to show any fear as he pulled the money from the bag to make sure it was all there.

"Okay, man. I trust you," Kap said, watching Pendleton pull the money from the bag.

"I have your back," Walter replied, glad that he'd agreed to the deal with Kap and thrilled that he was getting paid by both men without either being the wiser.

"A'ight."

"Don't forget about the added bonus for the detective on the case. We have to make sure all bases are covered and stick to our word. I think turning him on to a major drug deal in the process would be right down his alley. That will surely earn him the credits he needs to move up through the ranks," Walter said, smiling as he stacked the money on his desk.

"I got him. All he need to do is follow directions," Kap said, knowing that the drug deal would turn out to be a murder case instead. Kap hated to set Nikki up, but he needed her totally out of the picture just as much as he needed Yella dead. After all, his girlfriend was the only one who could sink him.

"Okay. I'm going to meet with the D.A. later, so you'll be all right. I will be in touch after everything is complete and official. I will personally deliver the paperwork to prove you are exonerated of all charges," Walter said as he placed the money back in the bag and pondered all the other arrangements he had in place.

"A'ight. I'll be in touch," Kap said. He exited the lavish office. Deep down, he regretted the deal he'd made, but staying free was his top priority.

As soon as he reached the car and positioned himself behind the wheel, his phone rang. "Hey! What up, baby?" he asked Nikki as he brought the car engine to life.

"Me and Yella headed out to the stash house. After we finish out here, we headed back out to my spot to freshen up," Nikki told Kap, knowing he'd read between the lines.

"What up, nigga! That county shit is fucked up. I thought y'all'd forgot about me!" Yella screamed from the passenger seat.

"Put 'im on," Kap told Nikki.

"Here," Nikki said, handing Yella the phone.

"Bro, you know it's on, and as far as that nigga B-Low, fuck him! We know the real. He wasn't trying to see us eat," Yella said, full of emotion and all cranked up as he relayed the same thoughts Kap had put in his head in the beginning so he would agree to crossing out B-Low.

"You dead right, my nigga. Fuck that nigga! Y'all go check the stash spot, and I'll catch up with y'all later," Kap told him as he fished a business card from his console.

"That's what's up, fam'!" Yella replied, then handed the phone back to Nikki.

"Yeah?" Nikki said. She was eager to get Yella out of the way to save her soon-to-be baby-daddy.

"Look, take that nigga to the back room and dead 'im on the spot. Don't play wit' 'im. Make sure he flat-line before you leave that bitch, you hear me?" Kap spat as he looked at the business card with Detective Green's name on the corner, right next to an official seal.

"Done. I'll get back with you later," Nikki said assuredly.

"Okay. Love you, boo," Kap told her.

"I lo…er, a'ight. See you later," Nikki said, almost slipping.

Kap ended the call, then dialed the number on the business card.

"Hello?"

"The address is 2736 Marcon Drive, Atlanta. She's on the way there now. The spot is full of enough product to get you that medal of honor. Our deal is done," Kap told Green, feeling some kind of way for setting up the woman who carried his seed.

Chapter 33

Real looked down at the strip of paper with Angelo's information on it and made sure he was at the right location before pulling the truck over to the curb. He glanced at the lakeside condo that sat perched on a hill, surrounded by acres and acres of well-manicured land and palm trees. Real pulled his Taurus PT92 and a flathead screwdriver from under the seat, then pulled on his black leather driving gloves. He didn't bother with his military fatigues or any other suspicious-looking clothing that might alert any witnesses to his real intentions. Dressed casually in a pair of jeans and a gray t-shirt, he stepped out into the night.

Angelo was finishing up his packing while his favorite TV show, *Shark Tank*, played on his fifty-six-inch flatscreen. Having carefully mapped out his plan, he made a call to his yacht captain and made sure they'd be ready to set sail in the morning. After confirming everything, he set the house up to look like he was going on a short vacation, a yacht trip; in reality, he was going on a very permanent vacation, running away from the life he used to love but now shunned in every way.

Real crept up outside the condo, looking for a good entry point. The place was designed in such a way that it was impossible to climb or enter through any one of the windows. Circling the house, he almost stumbled over the cliff that led down to an aggressive roaring river. "Shit!" Real cursed out loud as he regained his footing.

Doubling back, he noticed a side door that led into the condo utility room, which more than likely led into the kitchen or garage. Real pulled out his flathead screwdriver and slid it in the crack of the door. He wiggled it until it was wedged in enough to pop the lock, then gripped it tight and leaned in, putting pressure on it. On the second try, the door popped open, followed by the loud screeching of an angry alarm. "Fuck!" Real screamed.

He turned and took off, trying to get back to his truck, his adrenaline pumping like crazy. He glanced back over his shoulder and saw lights come on in the condo. By time he reached his truck, he saw other condos lights coming on. Just as he positioned himself behind the wheel of the truck, he heard sirens. Real pulled off slowly, careful not to draw any attention as he cruised down the dark, winding road, away from Angelo's spot.

Angelo grabbed his gun from his nightstand drawer as soon as the ADT alarm sounded. Checking the alarm pad on his bedroom wall, he saw that the intrusion had come at the utility room door, so he rushed out of the room and positioned himself at the top of the steps, waiting for the intruder to show. When he heard an engine roar to life, he turned and ran over to the window. He pulled the curtains back just in time to see a dark-colored truck driving away slowly. Minutes later, his whole street was lit up with flashing blue lights.

After talking to the police and checking out the utility room door, Angelo sat and thought for a minute about who might have been trying to break into his place. All kinds of thoughts ran through his mind: *The cartel, a burglar, some druggie?* That list of possibilities alone was all the affirmation he needed that it was time to move on and leave his current life behind.

Real pushed the truck to the other side of town. He decided to get a hotel room and try again tomorrow.

Chapter 34

"*L*et's make sure the last shipment all adds up," Nikki told Yella as they pulled up outside the dilapidated house they used to store their shipments of drugs when they arrived in the city.

"Now we can feed ourselves like we're supposed to without B-Low trying to chump us off with them crumbs," Yella told Nikki as he pushed his door open and exited the car, unaware of the plan Nikki and Kap had for him.

As they made their way inside, Detective Green was pulling up on the corner at the top of the hill of their street, positioning himself for a good view of the premises.

"We need to count up all this shit and figure out who owes us. Then I'll get with the connect so when we ready to re-up, we can go back to business as usual," Nikki said firmly as they made their way to the back of the house. She hadn't been to the stash house since the last drop-off, but right before B-Low had gone down, a shipment had come in. She and Kap had made plans to relocate it and start their own little operation. Stepping into the back room and seeing it empty took Nikki by total surprise, because she and Kap had specifically talked about moving the product only after they were situated and all packed to leave town. Now, standing in an empty room, she was stunned.

She knew it was time to finish Yella off, but she felt something just wasn't right about the whole situation. *Why didn't Kap say anything about moving the product? Did he move the product?* Her mind raced as she thought back on everything that had been going on. *Why was he stressing for me to put the money in his car at the house?* She stood there running the whole situation through her head when a loud *Crash!* came from the front of the house.

"What the hell?" Yella screamed as he made his way to the front of the house with Nikki on his heels.

"Freeze!" Detective Green called out, leveling his gun and pointing in their direction. Green smiled inside, knowing he was about to make the bust of the year. Kap had filled him in on the numerous blocks of cocaine stacked in the back room. Green was sure he'd be promoted with honors and would finally get that corner office he'd been working so hard for.

"Man, hold up! What the hell is going on?" Yella asked as he looked down the barrel of the man's gun, holding his hands up in the air.

"What the problem, Officer? Why are you in my house? We didn't call the police," Nikki said forcefully, trying to figure out why the detective was in the stash spot by himself with no back-up, acting like he had a guaranteed arrest on his hands. The more Nikki thought about it all, the clearer it got. *If I had killed Yella, he would have caught me red-handed. He busted in here like he knew something illegal was going down.* It was then that she realized Kap had set her up. Tears ran down her face as she thought about the man she loved betraying her.

"Look, man, just hold up. What's this all about?" Yella asked calmly, trying his best not to startle the detective.

In the split second while Yella was commanding Detective Green's attention, Nikki reached around and pulled her P-9 from the small of her back. Detective Green was caught totally off guard, for Yella's distraction had given her just enough time to get the drop on him. The *Boom*! from the P-9 pierced her ears. The first bullet hit Green in the shoulder, spinning him around, and the next one hit him in the back, blowing through to his chest. The impact of the bullets sent him reeling forward until he landed, face first, on the carpet.

"Shit, Nikki!" Yella screamed as he scrambled around the fallen detective.

"Let's go!" Nikki spat as she knelt down and snatched the detective's cell phone from his belt and stuffed it in her pocket.

"Damn, Nikki. You ain't have to blaze 'im, shit! We was clean," Yella choked out as he took off out of the house, with Nikki following close behind.

Just as they stepped out into the carport, a loud *Boom*! sounded, and Yella dropped like a ragdoll. The bullet had pierced the back of his head, splitting it open like a ripe watermelon.

"Snitch-ass nigga," Nikki spat as she stepped over him. As soon as she got in the car, she pulled the detective's phone from her pocket and looked through the call log. She wasn't surprised when she saw Kap's number listed as the most recent call.

B-Low waited patiently for Walter to show, and just like clockwork, his name was called. This time, Walter was already in the small glass visiting room before he arrived. He stood with his hands resting on back of the hard metal folding chair, and he was dressed in a pair of jeans and a button-down, most unusual attire for such a high-profile and expensive attorney.

"Hey, what up, Walter? We ready to sign them papers right?" B-Low said. It had taken him all night to build up the nerve to walk in there and sign away ten years of his life.

"We're just waiting on you. This deal is only on the table till tomorrow," Walter said firmly, turning to leave.

"Hold up, man. What the hell you talking about?" B-Low snapped as he walked up on Walter and blocked his exit.

"No money, no deal," Walter snapped back, hoping things wouldn't get physical.

"What the hell do you mean by that? I ain't paying you shit else. The half-million should be more than enough! You agreed to this shit, man. Ain't nothing else!" B-Low spat, trying his best to keep from punching the old man in the face.

"Yes, and I'm still in agreement with that, so when your friend calls and makes payment, we can move forward. However, as of right now, I haven't been paid," Walter explained as he slightly nudged B-Low out of the way.

"She ain't call you?" B-Low asked, surprised and shocked at the same time.

"No. I haven't heard from her. Just get in touch with me when you get your end together. Good day," Walter told B-Low as he stepped around him, pulled the door open, and stepped out. He needed B-Low to take care of the payment so he could get the deal done and free Kap from his charges. Walter had weighed the situation and decided to wait till the next day to make a decision on which way to go with everything.

As soon as B-Low stepped back into the pod, he rushed over to the phones. The pod had two phones. One wasn't working, and an inmate named Bo was on the other, having a heated argument with his baby-mama. "Bitch, fuck you. I wish you would try me!" Bo yelled into the phone.

B-Low stood back and waited for the phone to reach its fifteen-minute limit. In the middle of Bo screaming, the phone went out.

Disregarding B-Low standing to the side, waiting to use the phone next, Bo started dialing his baby-mama back.

"Yo, bro, I got next," B-Low called out, pissed that Walter hadn't been paid.

"Nigga, you right. You got next, but not till after I get finished!" Bo screamed as he turned to face B-Low. He had the phone to his ear and his face balled up. Bo was not one to be toyed with. He was six-two, 285 pounds of pure muscle. His hands were like small bricks, and he had battle scars all over him from his time in prison.

B-Low noticed all the cuts and bruises that lined Bo's face and bald head. After thinking about the whipping he'd taken downstairs in the holding cell, he decided to back down. "Check that, my nigga. You got it," B-Low told Bo as he walked away.

"Nigga, I know I got it!" Bo said, itching for B-Low to say anything he didn't agree with so he could take out all that anger on him—all the frustration from arguing with his baby-mama. Watching B-Low walk off, Bo turned back around and started back in on his baby-mama.

A minute later, B-Low was creeping back around with a mop handle and an attitude. B-Low crept up behind Bo as he screamed into the phone. B-Low knew every lick had to count, so when he swung the mop handle, he made sure it hit his target. It caught Bo on the top of his bald head, bringing blood instantly. The force of the blow caused Bo to drop the phone and grab his head. "Yeah, bitch-ass nigga! I know I got next!" B-Low screamed as he swung again, catching Bo square in the face and crushing his nose.

"Ahhhh!" Bo screamed, holding his face and head,

trying to get away from a deranged B-Low. Blood ran down Bo's face and head freely as he staggered over to the pod entrance, trying to get the officers' attention.

But B-Low didn't let up. He was right behind Bo, still beating him with the mop handle. "Don't run now, bitch!" B-Low screamed as he kept beating Bo in the head and back, until the big man folded up and went down.

The other inmates looked on, stunned. They'd heard about violent prison scuffles, but now they were seeing one live.

"Don't...you...ever...try...me! I'm...a...real...nigga!" B-Low stammered between blows.

Bo was out, curled up in a fetal position in a puddle of blood.

After tiring himself out, B-Low dropped the mop handle, kicked Bo in the face for the hell of it, and then made his way back over to the phone. He snatched the phone receiver up and dialed Nikki's number.

"The number you have reached..." said the automated voiced on the other end.

Low wanted to scream as the operator told him the number he was trying to reach had be changed or disconnected. He knew then that Nikki had gotten him good. She was gone, with all of his money and probably a bunch of his product. "Fuck!" he screamed, slamming the phone down. On his way back to his room, he noticed Bo slowly stirring on the floor, so he stepped back over and started kicking him crazily, taking all his anger out on him.

Finally, the officer on watch spotted the melee and

called a code for a fight. Minutes later, the pod was rushed by jailers, whipping out their tazers and hastily taking B-Low down. Medical personnel was called in for Bo, who was barely breathing, and the officers dragged B-Low downstairs to the restraining cell.

Chapter 36

The next day, Real was up early, heading back to Angelo's neighborhood in his truck. He wasn't sure if his Dodge had been spotted before, so he decided to park it down the block and walk back up to the condo. Real knew a random black man strolling through the predominantly white, upper-class neighborhood would raise a few eyebrows, so he picked up the pace and hoped he wouldn't be too noticeable. He banked on the fact that it was early and people would just be getting up.

Just as Real was coming up on the house, he saw Angelo's garage door opening up and a red Ferrari backing out. Wasting no time, Real turned and rushed back to his truck and took off in the same direction the Ferrari went.

Real caught up with Angelo at the bottom of the hill at a red light.

Angelo chatted away on his cell phone, paying no attention to the truck just outside his residence, the same truck he'd seen pulling away after the attempted break-in.

Real was real discreet in his pursuit. He stayed three cars behind the Ferrari as they made their way down the main highway. Real pulled his Glock .40 from his dashboard and laid it in his lap as he waited for a good time to end the chase.

Angelo just cruised along, unaware of the danger lurking just a few cars behind him.

Real decided to make his move at the next light. He sped up and got directly behind the Ferrari.

As they approached the light, Angelo made a detour onto Biscayne Boulevard.

Real noticed all the expensive yachts and other marine vessels lined up on the bay.

Angelo whipped the Ferrari into the harbor garage, still unaware of Real, who cruised on by.

Finding a parking space at the end of the commercial business strip, Real grabbed his Glock, stuck it under his shirt, and made his way back up to the building Angelo had parked beside. He entered the expensively furnished building like he was there to do business. As he made his way down a back hallway, he saw Angelo and another man turning the corner, coming in his direction. There was no way he could turn back.

"No problem, sir. Everything with your trip is worked out," Real heard the overweight, balding white man say as they approached.

Real quickly leaned down at the water fountain, hoping Angelo hadn't noticed or recognized him. If he had, Real would have no choice but to kill him on the spot. As they walked by, Real rose up and fell in a few steps behind them. He followed them outside to the dock.

The two paused in the middle of the dock as if they were waiting on someone. A few minutes later, they headed in the direction of Angelo's private yacht.

Real stood back and watched as Angelo and the man boarded the yacht. Then he casually walked over to the yacht, reaching under his shirt and pulling his pistol out.

Unfortunately, just as he reached the boarding ramp of the yacht, a young boy came running from the building. "Hey, mister! Hey!" the little boy screamed as he ran over to Angelo and the man with Angelo's bag in his hand. "You forgot your bag, mister!"

Real stopped in his tracks and rushed away from the yacht.

Angelo rubbed the small boy on the head, ruffled his hair, and thanked him for bringing him his bag.

Real waited for the coast to clear, then eased up on the yacht. He moved quickly, keeping his eye on Angelo and the man. After watching them disappear into the bottom level of the yacht, Real got out of sight long enough to pull his Glock from his waist again.

Just as Real started in, the man turned the corner and ran right into him.

"Oh, hey, buddy. Nice boat you got here," Real said, surprised by the man's sudden appearance.

"Yep, she's a beut', ain't she? But, uh, do I know you?" the man asked curiously.

"I was told I could find a man by the name of Angelo out here. Is he around?" Real asked as he slowly looked around to see if anyone was in sight.

"You're looking for Mr. Angelo? Well, he's, uh, in the restroom. Is there something I can help you with?" the man asked.

"Yeah, maybe. Step inside," Real said in a totally different tone as he pulled his gun and shoved the man into the captain's cabin..

"Huh? What? Hold on here. What's the problem, buddy? Can you just—" the man stammered, but he was cut off when the butt of the gun connected with the side of his head, sending him stumbling over the chair.

"Shut up and sit down," Real spat as he reached over and grabbed the hunting knife the man had strapped to his belt.

"Look, mister, whatever the problem between you and Mr. Angelo, I'm sure—"

"I said shut up and get in that chair!"

The man clumsily stood, picked the chair up from the floor, and sat down.

Real tucked his gun in his waist as he looked around for something to strap the man down. When he couldn't find anything suitable, he circled the man and readied the knife. In one swift motion, he reached over and grabbed the man by his forehead from behind. With his right hand, he came around and slashed the man's throat from ear to ear.

The knife slashed through his neck like hot butter, causing the man to grab at the wound frantically, as if he could somehow heal the two-inch gash that was now spurting blood. The man made two gurgling sounds, then fell over out of the chair.

Peeking out of the cabin, Real wiped the knife off,

tossed it aside, and headed downstairs to where Angelo was finishing up in the bathroom.

G STREET CHRONICLES
~A NEW URBAN DYNASTY~

WWW.GSTREETCHRONICLES.COM

*N*ikki rode around the city crying, lost in thought, and still stunned by Kap's betrayal. She had attempted to call him three times from the detective's phone, but he hadn't answered. After thinking things through, she picked the phone back up and texted him: "Need 2 C U. Urgent. Tks. 4 the info. Coin laundry, Godby Plaza. Got bonus 4 UR help." She knew how greedy Kap was, and she was sure he wouldn't hesitate to show for a bonus. She pulled up at the coin laundry on Godby Road to wait for him.

A minute later, he texted back: "We even now. B there in 10."

Nikki thought for a minute and decided she should move her car and park in the apartments across the street. By the time she was crossing the street, Kap was pulling up in front of the coin laundry. Nikki adjusted the brown paper bag that concealed her P-9. She walked through the parking lot casually, as if she'd just picked up a few things from the corner store. She eased up to the driver side of Kap's BMW, where he sat talking on his cell phone and smoking a blunt. Nikki's heart raced, not from the deed she was about to do, but from knowing she was about to watch the man she was completely in love with take his last breath. Tears rolled down her cheeks as she stepped up to the driver side door. Snatching her gun from the brown paper bag, she rushed up and stuck it in the window, catching Kap totally off guard.

"Shit! What? Whoa, girl!" Kap screamed out in panic, dropping his phone and the blunt as the cold barrel of the pistol rested on his temple.

"Nigga, you move, and I swear I'm pulling this trigger," Nikki shakily threatened through clenched teeth, her eyes watering.

"Baby, what you doin'? What's this all about? Come on now. Our li'l man inside of you got you tripping, that's all," Kap said, trying to soften Nikki up, realizing she was somehow behind the text message he'd gotten to summon him there.

"Don't even try it, Kap! How could you do this to me? I'm pregnant with *our* baby, nigga!" Nikki screamed, not caring about the homeless man who'd just walked up on the scene or the two drug dealers darting back and forth from the laundromat, serving the neighborhood fiends.

"Look, Nikki, you really tripping. You out here in broad daylight with a pistol to my head for no reason at all. C'mon, baby. Calm down and think about what the hell you doing," Kap said calmly, easing his unseen hand down to the .380 he kept in the pocket of his door.

"Naw, I ain't tripping! You betrayed me. Fuck you, Kap!" Nikki said, full of emotion.

It's now or never, Kap thought as he heard the venom in her voice. While going for his pistol, he slapped Nikki's pistol from his head, but it didn't take Nikki long to regroup. Just as she squeezed the trigger, Kap came out with the .380. Her first shot hit Kap in the stomach, and the other three tore into his groin, thigh and chest. Kap's one shot caught Nikki in her left breast, causing her to drop her pistol and retreat. Kap's blood drenched his brand new Gucci attire, but there was nothing he could do about it. He tried to cry out for help, but the sounds never came because of the thick, dark red blood that was now gushing from his mouth. Kap hoped it was all just some bad dream that he would wake up from any second. His breathing became faint, and his whole body felt as if it was on fire.

Out of nowhere, the homeless man from earlier appeared. He stuck his head in the passenger door and looked around the BMW like he'd left something in the car. He circled the car and picked up the P-9 Nikki had left behind.

Kap couldn't move or say anything. He only could watch as the man reached in through the back passenger window, pulled the money bag from the floor, and took off running. Kap took his last breath just as the man disappeared around the corner.

Nikki held her chest as she staggered back across the street to her car. By the time she reached her vehicle, she could hear emergency response teams coming in her direction. The last thing she remembered was police and paramedics surrounding her car, pulling her out.

Chapter 38

Real sat in the leather yacht recliner, quietly waiting for Angelo to exit the bathroom.

Minutes later, Angelo stepped out, drying his hands off on a wad of tissue.

"How's it going?" Real called out, cool and calm, toying with the gun resting in his lap.

"Wh-who are you?" Angelo asked, not even recognizing the man he'd been trying to kill for over a year.

"How about you have a seat and let's talk?" Real said with force as he picked the gun up from his lap.

"Look here, friend, you must be on the wrong boat. Could you—" Angelo's words cut off as Real pointed the pistol at him.

"Shut up and sit down!" Real snapped as thoughts of Constance and his cousin Max's deaths invaded his mind.

"Man, you got the wrong—"

"No, I've got the right one, Angelo. I know exactly who you are, and that's why I'm sitting on your million-dollar boat, about to blow your fuckin' head off," Real said heatedly.

Angelo eased down in the opposite leather recliner, finally realizing who the man sitting across from him was. He'd sent men at Real on various occasions, but the man in the photos looked nothing like the man who sat across from him now. Real's clean-shaven, youthful look had been replaced by a distressed, unkempt, stressful one. The fear seeped through Angelo's pores as Real stood. "Um... wait, Real. Look, we need to talk. I just—"

Real cut him off midsentence. "You sent your spic to kill me, huh? The same one who described in detail how he killed my lady on orders from you? It really touched me when he told me how he slashed her up and slit her throat at the end. He left her bleeding like a hog in the middle of the street," Real said, getting choked up as he looked at Angelo with pure hatred.

Angelo swallowed hard as he listened to Real explain Blanco's killing of Constance in graphic detail. "You... uh, you know, Real, I felt the same way wh-when my uncle was killed, but you...well, you know, in this business we...well, when it comes with the territory. You know, Real, I've heard a lot about you and know you are a man to be respected. With my connections and your hustle, we could make a lot of money. We've both lost someone we cared for dearly, so how about we call a truce and get back to what really counts for both of us... making money?" Angelo stuttered, keeping a close eye on Real as he started pacing the room.

"You are a clever man, Angelo, and I totally agree

with what you're saying—the money part, I mean. On the other shit, though, I really don't feel like we even yet. My cousin Max needs compensation. Do you agree?" Real asked with raised brows.

"I—" Angelo waited for Real to get in arm's reach as he paced the floor, then jumped up from the chair and shoved him as hard as he could.

Real stumbled over the opposite chair as Angelo bolted out of the cabin. Real hurriedly regained his footing and gave chase.

Angelo didn't hesitate. As soon as he reached the boat rails, he jumped head first into the cold, murky water.

Real was determined not to let him get away. Just as he started to heave himself over the railing, though, he noticed the deep sea fishing sphere mounted next to the rail. Real had prided himself as being one of the best when it came to using the sphere. Picking up the sphere reminded him of his last time out at sea with Constance and his old friend Pokey. Looking down into the water, he saw Angelo resurface and take off, fighting the current and trying his best to get out of Real's reach. Before he got too far off, Real readied the sphere and took aim.

Whoooooop! With lightning speed, the sphere caught Angelo right in the back of his neck, easily penetrating his soft neck tissue. The sharp pain that shot through his body didn't last long, and soon Angelo stopped stroking, his blood coloring the water around him.

When he saw that Angelo was motionless, Real turned and hurried back to the truck, satisfied.

Chapter 39

One Year Later...

Tino and Yaki walked around the prison grounds, talking about the encounter they'd had at GSCP two years earlier. After going head to head with the CERT team with knives, they'd been knocked down and put on high max at SSP until a month ago. Now they were out, plotting on their next move.

"I got to get me a flop, bro. Nigga feeling butt-ass naked around this bitch without an earpiece," Tino told Yaki as they walked around the prison yard, then discreetly slid through the yard gate and headed to the other side of the prison on a mission.

"Nigga, you know ain't nothing but a word. You know the rules of the land. You can't have it if you can't hold it," Yaki told Tino as they entered the other yard gate, then strolled over to the G building.

"Holla at Nutty for me, bro," Tino told a young thug

through the vent as he stood at the G building window.

"Nutty!" The young law-breaker screamed and threw his hand in the air, signaling to Nutty that someone was at the window for him.

Nutty was a good friend of Tino's from the east side of Atlanta.

Nutty slid over to the window in a wife-beater and flip-flops. "Shawty! What's popping? You just now comin' through to get at a playa?" Nutty said, displaying a mouth full of gold teeth. He looked exactly the same as he had years ago.

"Bro, you know how hard it is to get through the gate. Me and my nigga Yaki just got lucky they was slipping today,"

"What up, bro," Nutty said, acknowledging the big, hulking man who stood outside the window with his homeboy.

"What up, fam;," Yaki replied, leaning into the vent.

"Man, I was talking at my patna Slick, and he was around a nigga name Real who did some time a couple years ago. He was asking about a Tino and some nigga name Yaki," Nutty told them.

"You hollaed at my patna Real? Man, we ain't heard from homey since we went hard on the CERT team at GSCP. Do you got his info?"

"Yeah. He gave me his number to give to you. Boy, my people said he out there doin' his thang on a whole other level. They say this nigga moving heavy, bro, straight up. Hold up for a minute," Nutty told Tino as he stepped away from the vent and headed up to his room, holding his drooping pants up. A minute later, he was sliding Real's info through the vent.

"Who holding in this bitch, bro?" Yaki asked Nutty, bringing his face to the glass and using his hands to shield his eyes from the sun.

Nutty had been down long enough to know exactly what Yaki meant. "Flop or the green," Nutty asked, referring to cell phones and weed.

"Shit, both," Tino chimed in as he peered through the window too.

Nutty got close to the vent and replied, "Try 210, a nigga named Fatz, from Cobb County. Bitch-ass nigga been 'round here claiming the city, when he know he straight from the soft ass-out skirts. The li'l fat ho-ass nigga got a nice touch-screen phone, and he keep some of that loud on deck. My li'l patna started to get on him the other night, but as soon as they pulled up on the bitch, he instantly broke bread with the green. He knew his ass was on turn. What he do know, though, is that from that point on, he was gonna hafta keep paying to keep the young thugs off his ass," Nutty told them, leaning into vent.

"Who working over here?" Yaki asked, trying to see which officer was behind the control desk.

"Old lady Gilmore. Her old ass in the bathroom,"

"Get one of them li'l niggas to pop the door and let us in," Tino told Nutty.

Nutty turned and called for Li'l Trouble, his mission man.

When Trouble saw his mentor and role model calling, he hurried over, happy to be in the midst of some real prison vets.

"Look, go hit the button and let my nigga in while the old witch in the bathroom," Nutty told him.

"We'll holla," Tino told Nutty as he and Yaki headed for the front door.

Trouble eased over to the officer's desk and hit the button that opened the front door.

Seconds later, Yaki and Tino crept in. They didn't waste any time in moving through the dorm; they were on a mission.

A couple nosy inmates and some kiss-ass convicts who picked up on the negative vibes from the two out-of-place men walking fast through their dorm eased off to the side, positioning themselves for a better view. They stood back and watched the two men take the stairs two at a time and then head to the back of the dorm.

Yaki pulled Fatz's door open and stepped in, Tino following close behind.

"What…who…" Fatz paused as he looked back at the two unfamiliar men entering into his cell, closing the door behind them.

"Yo, shawty, you got that green for sale, don't you?" Tino asked from behind Yaki, noticing the fancy touch-screen Smartphone charging at the head of Fatz's bed.

"Shiiit, my nigga, we right on time," Yaki called out as he walked over and stood behind Fatz, who was sitting at the desk, sacking up a pound of loud.

It didn't take Fatz long to see what was about to go down. "Yeah, I got that good. What y'all boys trying to get? I'ma fuck wit' y'all wit' a killer deal," Fatz said, right before Yaki wrapped his tree-trunk biceps around his stubby neck and snatched him up and away from the desk.

"We trying to get it all, li'l bitch-ass nigga!" Tino called out as he grabbed the large bag of loud and raked what Fatz had sacked up back into the bag.

"Ai...aig...ughh!" Fatz choked out as Yaki held him with a tight grip.

"My nigga, grab that watch and that chain too, bro," Yaki told Tino. He watched him wrap up the cell phone and the charger and stuff it in his pockets.

"Boy, good eyes. I ain't even see dem," Tino said as he secured everything and then popped the door.

Yaki loosened his grip, but as soon as he did, Fatz swung wildly. He caught Yaki and dazed him.

As soon as Tino seen his partner stumble back, he set the bag down and stepped back in the room. Fatz rushed him, trying to flee the room, but Tino squared up at the door, blocking his exit. Fatz kept coming as Tino stepped back and timed his charge. Tino threw a hard right, standing Fatz straight up, and then followed up with a punch to the neck, taking Fatz's wind. As he was about to go hard on Fatz, Yaki was grabbing him from behind, snatching him to the back of the room.

All the commotion drew the attention of every prisoner in the dorm, as well as Mrs. Gilmore. "What's going on up there?" she asked Flip Mode, an old-school player from Atlanta who hated the nigga Fatz with a passion.

"Oh, they just wrestling and working out. They good," he assured her and smiled as she adjusted her thick, round glasses on her nose and went back to her desk to do her hourly logbook entries.

Yaki grabbed Fatz, slammed him to the floor, and beat him mercilessly in the face with his big, oversized hands. Fatz tried his best to try to get free from the big man's grip. Tino joined in and kicked him over and over, while Yaki pummeled him in the face until he was all bloody and unrecognizable. After he went out, Yaki and Tino busted out of the room, bloody and sweaty and hating that the sweet lick had taken so much effort.

"Let's go, bro! They gonna be locking the gate in a minute for count," Tino barked.

They tried their best to look normal as they made their way down the stairs.

Nutty saw them coming and went into action. "Mrs. Gilmore, a man can't breathe in here !" Nutty screamed, startling the old lady.

She jumped up and moved as fast as she could over to Li'l Trouble's room, where he was lying on the floor, faking.

Yaki and Tino watched her as she stood in the room doorway, trying to see what was going on. Tino strolled over to the desk and popped the button on the door so he and Yaki could make their exit. The loud *click* the door made caused her to turn around, but it was too late: Tino and Yaki were already headed back to the other side of the prison with Fatz's weed, jewelry, and cell phone in their possession.

Chapter 40

"ay, bro, this spot in banging. I'm loving this shit!" Chaz said over the new G-Spot woofers that were blasting Jeezy's new single.

"Yeah, playa! This place is a huge improvement over my last spot," Real replied as he looked around his recently opened, expensively decorated strip club on Peachtree Street in downtown Atlanta.

"Bro, you don't play. You got this spot right, real talk! I gotta tip my hat to you, fam'," Chaz told Real as the thick, heavily tanned, sexy Lightning caught his attention.

Real had made his way back to the top of the game since returning to Atlanta from his Miami trip. He and Kelly had become an item, and she was three months pregnant. Real was determined not to let his dream die, so he opened up another G-Spot. This time, instead of it being a four-star establishment, Real allotted a few more dollars and made it strictly five-star; only real ballers could afford to hang out there. Dances were $50 a song, and admission was double that. Real knew with those prices, the wannabe flexing trap stars wouldn't be in there taking up space. He'd rediscovered everything he'd lost: his car collection, mansion, and club. Real had it all except the one thing money couldn't buy, Constance. He thought about his baby girl daily. Kelly was a good woman, and he had grown to care for her deeply, but Constance still had his heart.

"I see you, boy. That's a beast of a white girl. Damn, Lightning," Real said. He laughed while she dipped down, showcasing her forty-six-inch backside.

Real had known Chaz for a minute, since they were both young niggas working their respective dope spots. They used to run in the same circle, but they'd never hooked up on business before. Chaz was a made man in his own right, but he wasn't getting it in like Real. After running into Chaz at the Velvet Room one night, Real invited him into his world. He needed a stand-up nigga on his team, a true hustler as well. Every since then, they'd taken over the South and were steadily moving their product to the East and West Coasts; they had become international.

"Damn, I gotta have me some of that. Excuse me, bro," Chaz said as he stepped away from Real and headed over to Lightning, who'd just finished her set with the old-school rich trick, Wadel.

Real was comfortable with Chaz being his right-hand man, but this time around, he was more cautious. He didn't want to relive another Cash or B-Low situation. Real had learned that to survive in the game, the only person he could trust was himself, period. Watching Chaz stroll over to Lightning, Real knew that one day, he'd be put in a compromising position because of his promiscuous ways. If Chaz didn't change, a woman was going to end up being his downfall.

Real looked at his watch and saw that it was nearing the time when he had to pick Kelly up from the airport. She'd been visiting her family more frequently since her Uncle Bink had been killed in a home invasion on the outskirts of Philly. She was the only one in her small family who could handle all his outstanding business ventures and investments.

Just as Real was headed out his cell phone rang. "Yeah?" he asked, not recognizing the unfamiliar number.

"The Real deal! What it is?" Tino called out, happy to hear his old partner's voice.

"Who? Tino? Boy, what it is?" Real stuttered when he recognized Tino's voice. He told Tino to hold on while he made his way out of the room so he could hear. Once he was away from the loud music, he closed his office door, sat behind his desk and spoke again. "Man, what's up?"

"Cooling, bro. Boy, I hear you out there making it happen," Tino said, watching Yaki sit at the desk in his room, sacking up the weed they'd taken from Fatz.

"Tell that boy Real I said what up," Yaki said, not looking up from the task at hand.

"Yaki says what up," Tino cut back in.

"Man, y'all two niggas together? Last I heard, y'all was both on lockdown."

"We was. We just came down. Ain't even been a month yet, but as you know, we making it do what it do,"

Tino said, motioning to Yaki to roll up a joint.

"Boy, I gotta get y'all boys something down there. I've been trying to get at you because I got a li'l problem down y'all's way," Real said, rearing back in his oversized, wing-backed, black leather desk chair.

"Problem? What kind of problem?" Tino asked, frowning up, trying to figure out what kind of problem Real could have in the joint since he was already out in the streets, doing it big.

"Nigga named B-Low just arrived at y'all's spot a while ago. I got at Nutty about this shit, but you know he ain't hands-on like that. I know y'all handle it for me," Real said in a serious tone, thinking about the grimy white girl Jessica, who worked for the Georgia Department of Corrections, his inside connect to all prisoners and their housing.

"Say no more, brother. We'll find out where he at, but what you want done?" Tino asked, ready to do whatever needed to be done.

"Don't kill the bitch-ass nigga. Y'all don't need no murder on your hands. Just make him wish he was dead," Real told Tino, knowing he would carry out the mission.

"I got you, bro."

After hanging up the phone, Real headed out of the club, en route to the airport to pick up Kelly. Twenty minutes into the ride, his phone beeped.

"Found the nigga. He over in J building. I'll be getting at you, bro," Tino told Real, letting him know the new arrival by the name of B-Low had been located.

"That's what's up! I got y'all, boys. Just hit me when

it's done," Real told Tino as he whipped his brand new Audi R-8 into the pick-up lane in front of the baggage claim.

"Gone," Tino said, ending the call.

Kelly rushed out of the airport when she recognized the black and chrome Audi pulling up next to the baggage claim.

Real got out and gave her a hug and a peck on the lips as he opened her door. "How was your flight, boo?" he asked as he put the Audi in drive and pulled off.

"Everything was fine. I'm just ready to get some much-needed rest," Kelly said as she pulled her phone from her purse and took it off airplane mode.

"I feel ya, boo. I'll drop you off before I head back down to the club to handle the rest of my paperwork."

"Please do. I'm so, so tired," Kelly said as her phone lit up alerting her that she had a text message. "What time can I come by?" the text read, bringing an instant smile to Kelly's face. Every since Real had got back on top, he and Kelly had been having it out about him not spending enough quality time with her. Their steadily deteriorating relationship consisted only of business calls and business meetings, and Kelly was way past fed up with it. She texted back, "He's going back out 2 the club. Come over. Make sure he's gone B4 U pull up."

The man on the other end waited restlessly for his phone to beep with Kelly's response text as he sipped on a small glass of Hennessy Black. As his phone lit up displaying Kelly's text, he rubbed his hard-on thinking about how good she always put it on him—not to mention her, as he called it, *monster head game*. He couldn't hold back the smile as he thought about his seed growing in her. Chaz gulped the rest of the Hennessy down hurriedly, exited the club, and headed out to Kelly's.

Chapter 41

B-Low had been at SSP, one of Georgia's maximum security prisons, after being transferred
from the medium security JSP due to his maximum security
status. He'd been sentenced to life in prison for murder, and
the federal charges Walter had been paid to erase somehow
resurfaced. B-Low was also tried and sentenced to an ad-
ditional twenty years in federal prison. Walter had left him
high and dry after Nikki had run off with all of his money.
Sitting in trial with Charlie Chew, the worst indigent defense
attorney in the state of Georgia, B-Low knew he didn't stand
a chance. When the judge handed down his life sentence, all
he could think about was Nikki and making her pay. Every
day he sat in the small, hot, cramped cell only fueled the fire
for his revenge.

Sitting in the prison dorm dayroom, B-Low looked
around to see if he knew any of the men who were suffering
the same fate at the hands of the cruel Georgia court system.
He picked up an old magazine from the dayroom table and

started flipping through it. He glanced up and noticed two Muslim inmates donning bright white kufis, traditional Muslim headgear. They were on the top level, pointing at him. A hard tap on the shoulder from behind slightly startled him.

"Yo, B-Low. What it do, homey?" Malachi, a former gang-banger turned Muslim from Atlanta called out as he held up his closed fist for some dap.

B-Low didn't recognize the man, but right off the top, he realized he was Muslim because he wore a kufi over his clean-shaven bald head. He instinctively looked back up at the other Muslims who were pointing at him. B-Low knew it would be good to be down with the Muslims while he was locked up, because they were like one big family who looked out for each other, no matter what. "Wh-what up, bro?" B-Low replied, not recognizing the man but playing along. He'd decided he wanted to join the band of men, even if it meant changing his religion.

"Boy, I thought that was you. Shit, look here. I gotta holla at my two brothers up here right quick. I'll get back at ya in a minute," Amin told B-Low as he looked up and gave his other two Muslim brothers on the top range a confirmation nod. They, in turn, ducked off into a cell and called Tino on their cell phone.

"He in here, bro. What's the move?" Hasad asked Tino, who tapped Yaki on the shoulder.

Yaki looked up from the desk, where he was still sacking up the weed they'd taken from Fatz.

"Hold on," Tino told Hasad, his good friend and once his partner in crime years ago at ASP, a prison in Augusta,

Georgia. "Say, peeps, which way you wanna play this nigga B-Low?" Tino asked Yaki.

Yaki looked up at the ceiling in thought, then answered, "Get 'im to the gym and Charles Black that nigga," Yaki answered, referring to one of Atlanta's most respected made men and the punishment inflicted on one of the men who robbed him.

"Oh shit! Yeah, okay. In the rec' pen. I'll holla at Peaches. I know we can hit that sissy-ass nigga with a fifty of that green, and he'll be down," Tino said. He was tripping on Yaki's suggestion, but he totally agreed because it fell right in line with what Real had told them: "Make him wish he was dead." Tino turned his attention back to Hasad, who was patiently holding the line. "Yo, bro, get the nigga up to the gym in the morning."

"You don't want us to smash this nigga?" Hasad asked, ready to put some work in for his old partner.

"Naw. We got 'im. Just trick his ass up to the gym in the morning," Tino told him as Yaki passed him the fat joint.

"A'ight. Got you, bro," Hasad said, then ended the call.

Thirty minutes later, all the Muslims were sitting at the table with B-Low, making him feel right at home.

Chapter 42

$\mathscr{P}$ulling up at his million-dollar Mediterranean-style home nestled amidst acres and acres of a well-manicured lot, Real waited for Kelly to get out of the car. Then he pulled out his cell phone and called Bradley, his police connect. "It's on you now," Real told him after Kelly grabbed her tote and got out of the car without a goodbye or a see you later.

"I see you," Bradley said in an official tone, watching Real pull out of his driveway and speed off.

Not a good five minutes later, another car pulled up. Bradley sat in his Dodge van in the driveway of the foreclosed house across the street. He watched the man get out of his new Acura NSX and head up to the door. Bradley pulled out his camera and snapped a couple pictures, then picked up his cell phone and called Real. "Damn. Lady don't waste no time, I see," Bradley said while watching the man exit the car.

Real had been real suspicious lately because of Kelly's

sudden departures and her lack of interest in sex. Kelly hadn't been herself for the last month, and Real knew something wasn't right. At first he blamed it on her pregnancy, but after picking up her phone and seeing that it was locked, he knew she was up to no good. Instead of jumping the gun without proof, Real called his old police connect, Bradley, and told him to watch her for a week after she got back in town.

"What's up? What you see?" Real asked, his blood starting to boil.

"Well, she just opened the front door for a nice-looking guy and gave him her tongue for keeps. They went in, most likely about to fuck each other's brains out in your nice, comfortable bed. One thing I can say is that the guy got nice taste in cars, because his bright orange Acura NSX is beautiful," Bradley said, checking out the customized flashy car.

Real turned his Audi R-8 around in the middle of the street and punched the gas. He knew the only bright orange, customized NSX in the city—or the state, for that matter—belonged to Chaz, his right-hand man.

"I'm on my way," Real said as he tossed his phone in the passenger seat.

Bradley couldn't reply before the line went dead. He cranked up the van and pulled out of the driveway away from the scene, just in case it turned into a homicide. He knew Real all too well. He figured he'd just call him later to find out what happened.

* * *

"Man, I need to start studying that Koran. I've always thought about changing my religion to Muslim. See, most of my family is Muslim, so I might as well join them. What I need to do?" B-Low lied, looking for any kind of way to get closer to the group of men who looked out for each other like brothers.

The men around the table weren't at all impressed or fooled by his words. They all smiled, kicked it, and played right along.

"Your decision to embrace the ways of the Koran is a good one. As a matter of fact, you should come with us to the gym in the morning to meet a couple of the other brothers and our Imam," Hasad told him, casting his other two brothers sideways looks that B-Low didn't pick up on.

"Okay. That's what's up. Y'all straight? I got some chips and other shit they don't sell in the store down here," B-Low offered, trying to seal his fake friendship deal with the brothers.

The brothers were really disgusted with B-Low's cowardice, but they'd seen his kind before. Many men had supposedly denounced their various religions just to get down with the Muslim community for the sake of protection; B-Low's game was nothing new to them.

"Naw, we straight, bro. Just make sure you're up and ready in the morning," Hasad said as he and the other two brothers got up to head to their room.

"I'll get with y'all boys in the morning," B-Low called.

He stood and returned to his room, where someone had broken into his locker box and stolen all his commissary and electronics.

"Make sure that coward-ass ho is up bright and early," Hasad told the brothers

B-Low rushed out of his room and up the stairs in their direction.

"What up, bro?" Hasad asked a frantic B-Low just as he was about to step into his room.

"Man, somebody done broke in my shit, my nigga!" B-Low said, all hyped up and looking around the dorm, trying to spot anything suspicious.

"What? We don't even rock like that, bro, but look... it's about time for lockdown for the count, so let's just lie low till morning. As soon as we get back from the gym tomorrow, we'll free pick one of these niggas and make an example out of him, straight up," Hasad said in a way that had his other two brothers discreetly giggling.

"That's what's up! These niggas done fucked up now," B-Low screamed across the dorm, causing everyone to look up at him as he made his way back downstairs.

When Hasad got back to his room, he grabbed a pack of Skittles out of the bag that Booman, the dorm thief, had placed on his bed. Whenever a lick was pulled off in the dorm, Hasad always got a cut.

Chapter 43

$\mathscr{R}$eal pulled up in his driveway and abruptly killed the engine on the Audi, hoping Kelly and Chaz hadn't heard him. He grabbed his Colt .357 off the seat, got out, and headed up to the door. The two people he trusted most had betrayed him in the worst way. Real didn't take it hard though; from past experiences with close friends, he knew there was always a chance to be crossed. From his old right-hand man Cash to his partner B-Low, Real had learned not to trust anyone but himself.

As he made his way up to the door, he thought about what he had hanging over his head. Kelly knew about Blanco's death, and that could surely get him sent back to prison. Chaz knew about most of his operations and could do him a lot of damage. The people inside weren't as loyal as he'd taken them to be, and he had only one option.

When Real opened the door, he noticed Kelly's clothes strewn throughout the front room. Real took in each piece of her clothing, all the way down to her bright red thong. As he got closer to the bedroom, he heard moans and cries. He stepped over to the door and put his ear to it, unaware of the figure behind him with a 12-gauge pistol-grip pump extended in his direction.

"Nigga, drop it," Chaz said coolly and calmly, nudging the pistol into Real's back.

"So this how it is, nigga?" Real asked, dropping the Colt to the floor, furious that he'd been caught slipping.

The moans stopped on cue, and Kelly stepped out, dressed in a pair of tight-fitting jeans and three-inch heels, pulling her Gucci luggage behind her. "Chaz, I'll be in the car," she said as she walked by and looked Real up and down through her Gucci frames.

"So this is what it come to? Say, you fuck-ass bitch!" Real screamed, so boiling mad that spit flew from his mouth as he yelled.

"Nigga, shut the fuck up and let's get to the safe. Next time, don't make it so damn obvious that you're watching me," Chaz said, pushing Real in the back with the pistol-grip pump.

"In the office, under the desk!" Kelly screamed as she opened the door to exit.

"Look, man, we've known each other too long for this shit here. Bro, it ain't gotta go down like this," Real grumbled as he walked to his office at gunpoint.

"Yeah, I feel you, my nigga. See, I could take yo' life, but since we go way back, I'm gonna let you live. Just let me get the money, and we good," Chaz said, knowing that as soon as the safe was open, Real was dead.

Real knew it too, because Chaz wouldn't live twenty-four hours if he left Real alive to deal with him. Real would come at him full speed, no questions asked. As Real made his way to the back of the office, he thought of a way to change the current situation. He entered the office, walked over to his desk, and slid it over a couple of inches, exposing the digital safe beneath it.

"Nigga, hurry up!" Chaz screamed, getting fidgety, ready to be up out of Real's spot.

"Hold up, man. I'm going fast as I can," Real said, measuring the distance of the 12-gauge Chaz had made the mistake of holding way too close to him. As soon as Real bent down, he hit the alarm on the safe. The loud screeching sound instantly grabbed Chaz's attention, which gave Real the half-second he needed to make his move. Real rose up, swung around, and knocked the barrel of the 12-gauge away from him. He then grabbed the much smaller Chaz and kneed him between the legs, instantly crippling him.

"Ah!" Chaz screamed as he tried to hold on to the 12-gauge, which Real was now easily commanding from his grip.

"Don't fold now, bitch nigga!" Real called out as he took possession of the gun and shoved Chaz hard as he could, sending him stumbling backward into the wall. Real lifted the gun and pulled the trigger.

Boom! The slug put a big, gaping hole in the center of Chaz's chest.

Chaz stared wide-eyed at Real as he coughed up blood, took his last breath, then slid down the wall to the floor.

Wasting no time, Real rushed through the house to get to Kelly, who was out front, behind the wheel of the idling NSX, waiting on Chaz.

Kelly spotted Real coming her way full speed, carrying the 12-gauge. "Shit!" she screamed as Real lifted the gun. She threw the car in drive and hit the gas, burning rubber out of the driveway, with Real only a few feet behind.

Not about to let her get away, Real pulled the trigger, shattering the back window of the car. The NSX was too fast, though, and he knew it was no use trying to catch her. "Bitch!" he screamed, as if she could hear him, and then he turned back and headed inside.

He knew the police would be arriving soon, especially with the alarm going off. He struggled to get his story together before they arrived.

Moments later, police in both marked and unmarked cars whipped into his driveway after being alerted by the alarm call center.

Real walked out and greeted them. "Thank you for coming, Officers," Real explained. "He's inside," he said, letting them know where the intruder was.

"We'll take it from here," Bradley said, giving Real an I-got-you nod as he and the uniformed officers headed into the house.

Chapter 44

" $\mathcal{G}$ ym call! Gym call! You got five minutes to report out!" Officer Swint screamed from the front of the dorm, alerting all inmates of the early-morning recreation period in the gym.

"Yo, B-Low!" Hasad screamed as he and the other two brothers rushed down the stairs, ready to lead B-Low to his fate. Hasad and the other two wanted to straight-up smash B-Low. They hated his slick, wannabe, cowardly ways.

"Yeah, I'm on deck, waiting on y'all," B-Low replied. He was already standing by the door, ready to head out.

As they rounded the sidewalk and entered the gym, Hasad spotted Yaki, Tino, and a couple more of their partners in the workout pin in the far corner, lifting weights. "Yo, yo, homey!" Hasad called out, directing his entourage over to the workout pin where Yaki, Tino, Cooly, and the sissy Peaches stood.

"Boy, what's up, my guy?" Yaki called out when they

walked into the pin.

"Man, we just kicking it, trying to show my patna B-Low here the ropes on this prison shit. What y'all boys up to?" Hasad said, giving Tino the nod.

Tino stepped out of the pin, looked around to make sure the coast was clear, then stepped quickly back in, purposely blocking the doorway. As soon as Yaki saw Tino in place he walked over close to B-Low. Hasad, Peaches, and the other two brothers stepped back, recognizing the move.

B-Low stood there looking around, listening to the idle conversation between the men. He was so excited to be there that didn't even notice Cooly and Yaki pulling up on him.

Cooly looked at Yaki, who, in turn, frowned and advanced on an unsuspecting B-Low.

"Ma-mannn! Ah!" B-Low screamed as Yaki's big fist connected with the side of his head, knocking him over into the side gate of the pin.

"Yeah, fuck nigga!" Cooly screamed as he followed up, landing solid blows to B-Low's shocked face.

"Man, hold up! What's up wit' y'all! Come on, man!" B-Low screamed, hoping for help, unsuccessfully trying to dodge the blows the men were throwing his way.

Tino pulled the eight-inch blade from his jacket, prompting Hasad and the other two brothers to leave. "Grab that hoe-ass nigga! Put him face first on the bench and strap 'im down!" Tino yelled while looking around to make sure the coast was still clear.

The few inmates participating in morning rec' saw

the commotion, but they just looked the other way, not willing to get involved or serve as witnesses.

B-Low didn't know what was going on. He looked around for the brothers, hoping it was just some kind of Muslim initiation or just a cruel joke. "Man, please! What's this all about?" B-Low asked as they manhandled him and slammed his face down on the weight bench.

Tino walked over and grabbed a bag from the corner. It had three rolls of clear tape in it, as well as two torn sheets platted into a long rope. "Strap him up," Tino told Peaches, handing him the bag of supplies.

"Man fu—"

Smack!

Cooly and Yaki kept up with their assault, keeping a squirming B-Low subdued.

"Damn it! Hold 'im down, fellas!" Peaches called out like a girl. He then walked over and started wrapping the rope and tape around B-Low and the bench.

Minutes later, B-Low found himself helplessly tied and taped to the bench, face down and unable to move. "Ah! Help! Help!" he yelled, but was quickly silenced by a strip of tape roughly strapped across his mouth.

"Where the razor? Hurry the fuck up!" Tino screamed at Peaches, who was now digging in the bag frantically, looking for the open razor.

"I got it right here. Damn, boy. Give a bitch a li'l time, baby," Peaches said as he walked over and got behind B-Low.

"Mmm! Mmmm!" B-Low squirmed around, fear written all over his face.

Peaches took the razor and split the back of B-Low's pants, then carefully put a slit in the back of his boxers.

B-Low, totally lost to everything that was going on, looked with pleading eyes from Tino to Yaki, then over to Cooly.

"Bitch nigga, ain't no need to be looking crazy now! You wasn't looking crazy when you crossed my nigga Real," Tino said with attitude, taking in the crazed expression at the mention of Real's name.

"Mmm! Mmmm! Mmmmmm!" B-Low threw his head from side to side, thrashing his body around like a madman, but the tape and ropes only allowed him to move so far.

Peaches had B-Low's buttocks completely exposed. He looked from Tino to Yaki, then smiled as he leaned down and kissed B-Low's exposed butt cheeks. He then unbuckled his belt and pulled his way-too-tight pants down.

"Yo, Peaches, make sure you see blood. We gonna be posted out here by the door to make sure everything cool," Tino said as he turned and walked off, with Cooly and Yaki in tow.

"Don't you worry, boys. I got this," Peaches said as he mounted B-Low. "I'm gonna love him real good."

Before they reached the door, they heard a loud, muffled scream. Tino looked back and saw Peaches behind B-Low, slamming his hard erection in and out of him roughly. Peaches tore into B-Low time after time. On the fourth stroke, he saw blood, which substituted for a lubricant. He began pumping furiously, sliding in and out of B-Low with ease.

B-Low's veins were about to burst in his forehead as tears of anger and pain flowed down his cheeks. He would have rather been dead than where he was, and that was the plan all along.

It only took Peaches five minutes to come to a climax, successfully passing on the HIV he'd contracted while selling his body on the mean streets of Atlanta.

After gym call was over, Officer Lance made his rounds to make sure all the inmates had returned to their respective living units. As soon as he entered the workout pin, he threw up. The smell of blood, sweat, shit, and sex turned his stomach. He fumbled with his radio as he called for assistance in the gym.

A few minutes later, B-Low was being cut loose and carted to medical.

The warden was called in to assess the situation, but B-Low was in so much shock that he couldn't speak. "When he gets back from the hospital, lock 'im down and put him in a transfer," the warden told the captain as he exited the room, not really interested in the everyday occurrences that took place at SSP.

Chapter 45

Six Months Later…

"*D*amn, where the players and ballers at? Scandalous need $50 more to take it all off!" Loo, the G-Spot MC screamed as the tall, thick, black dime-piece moved her body to the beat of Future's new smash hit.

Since the shooting at his spot, Real had been lying low. He'd found out through his street connects that Kelly had left town and had lost the baby. Things in the street had been going real well. He'd scaled back on his shipments and was a one-man show now; he liked it better that way. The money wasn't as plentiful, but at least he didn't have to worry about the greed and envy bullshit that came with having a crew. Besides, the club was bringing in major dough.

Real still thought of his baby girl, Constance, on a regular basis. She was the one and only person he'd ever been able to trust with his life. At times, he replayed his life and constantly blamed himself for her death. Walking through the club, he thought back on all the good times.

He entered his office and pulled out his desk drawer, from which he retrieved a small pouch containing some of the best cocaine money could buy, along with a small straw. He dumped a small mountain of the potent drug on his desk. He placed the straw in the middle of the mountain and took a big heave in each nostril. "Ah, shit!" Real called out as the cocaine invaded his body instantly.

Knock! Knock! Just as he was about to dig into the mountain again, there was a knock at the door.

"Yeah?" Real screamed. He grabbed a piece of his desk stationery and placed it over the straw and cocaine.

"Can I come in?" Desire asked.

"Come on," Real replied as he moved the paper and took another hit.

"Damn. Can I get down?" Desire asked. She was a half-black, half-Latina dime-piece who coulda passed for one of Kim Kardashian's sisters. She sashayed over to Real's desk and placed one ass cheek up on the corner, right next to the mountain of powder.

Real didn't respond verbally; he just handed her the straw. As she leaned down to hit the powder, exposing all of her goods, Real reminisced on the last time he'd sexed her. Desire was the true definition of a beast in bed. Every since Kelly's departure, Real had resorted to sleeping with a number of the G-Spot dancers, which was totally against his own rules. Things had changed, though, and the best way for Real to deal with it all was through drugs and a high-powered sex life. Strangely though, the more he partied, got high, and got off—all the things the young thugs in the streets chased after—the more he realized that life wasn't all that great.

"Oh fuck yeah! This is some good shit, Real!" Desire called out as she leaned her head back and squeezed her nose.

BAM!

Real's office door flew open, and a gang of Atlanta police and GBIs rushed in.

"Get down! Get down now!" the leading officer barked. He was dressed in plain clothes and a bullet-proof vest.

Desire wiped the powder from the desk as she stood, then lowered herself to the floor.

"What the fuck is this all about?" Real asked as he lowered himself to his knees, completely high off the cocaine.

"Richard Walker, you have the right to remain silent," the old veteran detective called out as he made his way through the crowd of officers who held their weapons steady and pointed at Real.

"Man I ain't did shit to break the law, so could you all please exit my place of business?" Real said calmly, feeling the effects of the cocaine rush through his body.

"You are under arrest for the murder of Tina Crumb. Now put your hands behind your back," the detective yelled as the uniformed officer rushed and cuffed him.

Real thought for a minute, and then it hit him. *Tina!* He reflected back on the day in the hotel room when he'd been fresh out of the joint, high on cocaine and liquor.

He replayed the day. He had blacked out and beaten that junkie trick until she was all swollen and bloody; now he finally knew her fate. Out of all the killing and murders he'd been involved in, he couldn't believe he was being arrested for the death of a crack-head prostitute. He didn't even know he'd accidentally committed that murder.

"I just love DNA," the detective said jokingly as they lifted a handcuffed Real to his feet and led him from the club.

As soon as the officers cleared the office with Real, Desire searched Real's desk and took everything of value. "Yeah, Real…some good shit!" she said, happily grabbing everything she could carry.

* * *

Real placed all his property in his small, cramped cell and stepped back into the dorm that housed 120 men. CSP was one of Georgia's most violent prisons, and 99 percent of the men housed there would never walk free again. Real swore he would fight his conviction till the end, but deep down inside, he knew it was over. As he looked around the dorm, he realized and accepted the fact that the prison would be his final home.

He pulled his Bible out and removed the envelope he'd stuck inside it, the one in which he'd placed the last picture he and Constance had had taken together. He closed his eyes while a tear ran down his cheek. He thought back on the day they'd held each other, smiling and acting silly, while the friendly Jamaican snapped picture after picture. Real sat on his bed and thought about the life sentence he'd been handed down two months ago by the racist judge.

As he unpacked, he heard some ruckus outside in the dorm, and he couldn't believe his eyes when he looked to see what was going on. Three men were jumping on another one, sticking and beating him at the orders of a fourth man. Real knew that whoever the man was giving the orders, he had to be a powerful and dangerous man. He'd served time before, and Real knew he needed to do his homework and find out who the man was.

Just as he was about to go downstairs to get a closer look, he noticed the man looking up in his direction. Real stared right back at the man, knowing that breaking a stare in prison would have everyone considering him weak. After successfully staring the man down, he stopped on the steps.

B-Low squinted and glared up at the familiar man coming down the steps. He walked over to the steps to get a closer look. He couldn't believe he'd run back into Real again after all those years. B-Low called out to his gang members while Real reached down and strapped his shoes up tight.

It had been a long day for Real, lying in his bed replaying the day's events.

At lockdown time, the guard locked all of the doors, then went to the middle of the floor and announced, "Lights out!"

Real stared up at the ceiling as blood seeped from the large wounds from the long handmade knives the gang-bangers carried. After seeing B-Low, he'd immediately rushed back to his room, but he didn't have time to close his door. B-Low and the other bangers rushed in the room and stuck him unmercifully, until he blanked out. When he woke up, he noticed they'd placed him in the bed under the covers. He tried to move but couldn't; he had lost too much blood, and it felt like his leg was broken. He tried to scream, but nothing came out. So, Real just stared at the ceiling in the dark, knowing it really was over.

The guard looked around the dorm and made the announcement again: "Lights out, boys! Lights out!"

Fake ID, filing fraudulent income tax returns, credit card fraud, going on Twitter and Facebook with fake donation scams and Feed the Hungry campaigns…Yandi, Pinky and Precious were three friends that were out to get theirs by all means necessary with the computer as their main tool.

What happened to honor amongst thieves?

Just when money was stackin' and things were looking up, the unthinkable happened and the lives of these three woman spiraled out of control. CB and Mookie held a deadly secret and the feds sent a man in to bring down the operation, but what happens when their own wants a piece of the 10 million dollar payday?

Now the women have to make a deadly decision that's going to cost someone close to them or they're going to lose all they had, including their very own lives. A decision had to be made and fast.

Who would've thought Hackin' & Stackin' could go so wrong!

The Drama Series
George Sherman Hudson

GEORGE SHERMAN HUDSON

GEORGE SHERMAN HUDSON

We'd like to thank you for supporting G Street Chronicles and invite you to join our social networks. Please be sure to post a review when you're finished reading.

Facebook
G Street Chronicles
&
G Street Chronicles "A New Urban Dynasty" Readers' Group

Twitter
@gstrtchroni

My Space
G Street Chronicles

Email us and we'll add you to our mailing list
fans@gstreetchronicles.com

George Sherman Hudson, CEO
Shawna A., VP